I0557424

The Wylder Rose

by

Jane Lewis

The Wylder West Series

The Wylder Rose

Cover Art by *Tina Lynn Stout*

The Wild Rose Press, Inc.
PO Box 708
Adams Basin, NY 14410-0708
Visit us at www.thewildrosepress.com

Publishing History
First Edition, 2022
Trade Paperback ISBN 978-1-5092-4127-9
Digital ISBN 978-1-5092-4128-6

The Wylder West Series
Published in the United States of America

Dedication

For my brave, beautiful, strong, and kind niece,
Rebecca.

Chapter One

Wylder, Wyoming
April 1879

Callum MacPhilip angled his head so the brim of his Stetson would block the oppressive snow and enable him to see the road. The powerful wind blew a haze of ice on the exposed skin of his face, neck, and ears. He hunched over so his body would fall toward the warmth of the horse and shivered while the strong Clydesdale trudged through the snowdrifts toward the ranch. The freak storm ended his poker game at the Five Star Saloon and halted his plans to spend time with Amethyst at The Wylder County Social Club. Responsibilities at the Lex Taylor Ranch propelled him through the early spring storm.

Daniel Taylor, his best friend and previous employer, offered him a partnership in the ranch after Daniel married Sarah, and he accepted. Not much changed except his name on some papers and an increase in his salary. He'd loved the ranch since they arrived in Wylder near six years past. Daniel bought the land and Callum accepted the job as a ranch foreman and horse trainer. Together they raised and sold the best quarter horses in Wyoming. Callum planned to expand the herd to Clydesdales. A Scotsman, he favored draft horses and today he was thankful for the strong stallion and how the horse navigated the snow drifts and impassible winds with ease.

He didn't notice the horse and buggy until Icefall stopped and sniffed at the almost frozen horse. He slipped off his mount and used the carriage horse for guidance to the buggy. A small still figure lay in a fetal position on the seat. Fear climbed up his spine as his gaze swept over what appeared to be a lady dressed in a long black woolen cloak. "Are ye all right?" he called over the ferocious wind.

A limp arm draped over the edge of the seat, her pale skin exposed to the freezing air above a gloved hand. He placed his fingers on her wrist and detected a faint pulse. "I'll take care of ye."

The Scotsman worked from experience instead of sight. He unhitched the horse and tied the reins to Icefall's saddle horn. The wind and snow battered him on the way back to the carriage where he scooped the woman in his arms. She was dead weight, and he steadied himself against the gusts of wind to fight his way to the draft horse. He placed her on the tall animal and mounted holding her close. The wind blew the snow in his face and the carriage horse resisted until Icefall tugged the stubborn animal like a heavy log. Callum bent his head toward the snow-covered ground and called to his stallion. "Take us home."

The journey was slow, but Icefall performed his duty and plodded to the lane. He approached Daniel and Sarah's house and stopped beside the bell. He slapped the clapper against the steel several times until the front door opened.

Daniel held onto the rail as he descended the steps. "Red, are you all right?"

"Aye, cold but I rescued a lass on my way back from town. She's in bad shape, and I need to see to her welfare. This is her horse. We'll worry about the carriage after the storm. I'm near froze meself." He untied the straps to the mare and passed them to his friend.

Daniel grabbed the reins. "I'll get this girl to the barn."

Callum guided Icefall to his house and dismounted with the woman in his arms. The hood of her black cape hid her face, and a fear she would not survive settled in his bones. An enormous snowdrift blanketed the area, which caused him to lose his balance. Unable to hold her in his arms and make it through the piles of snow, he threw her over his shoulder and held onto the porch rails. They entered the house where he placed her on a rug before the fireplace.

He hurried to his bedroom and grabbed all the quilts from his bed and covered her. With the strike of a match, kindling ignited the wood and the fire roared to life. Heat radiated out to warm the front room. After an inspection of the lass to assure himself she was alive, Callum raced out the front door to see to Icefall. The horse was gone. He focused on movement through the fog of snow and saw the outline of Daniel guiding the Clydesdale to the barn. He yelled over the wind. "Need any help with the horses?"

Daniel waved. "I've got it. Need any food?"

"No. Got to see to this lass is all." Callum entered his home, lit several kerosene lamps, and gathered pillows.

The woman lay still. He snuggled a pillow under her head and placed his fingers along the side of her neck. The pulse of the blood through her veins was too weak for his liking. Her red wavy hair fought to escape the hood of her wool cape and resurrected a memory. He turned her face toward the light of the fireplace, a recollection of the woman as she stepped into a carriage with an older man hit him like an upper cut to his chin. Every visit to Cheyenne had him searching for this woman.

She opened her eyes. "Walker?" Her voice was soft as a kitten mewing.

"No, lass. I'm Callum MacPhilip. I found ye almost froze on Old Cheyenne Road. I'm going to care for ye." He raised the quilt from her legs and tugged off her boots and stockings. Her feet were blue from lack of circulation and cold as a block of ice. A check of her clothes found them wet from her dress to her bloomers. He undressed her and piled the quilts on top of her body, then placed her clothes close to the fire to dry.

"I can't feel…my…" Her voice faded and her body stilled.

Panic stabbed his gut like a boning knife. He fell to his knees and put his hand on her neck. The beats grew weaker, and her body shivered. Desperate to warm her, he stripped his clothes from his body and joined her under the quilt. His feet embraced hers and his hands cradled her ice-cold fingers while her body rested under his, absorbing the body heat. Her breathing was shallow, and he held his breath while listening, praying, and hoping she wouldn't die.

Hours passed with the lady secure in his arms. Moments ago, her body stopped shivering and she'd snuggled onto his shoulder. With her cradled on his arm and the awareness she was out of danger, her soft body and the smell of her rose-scented hair stirred his arousal. Jesus, Mary, and Joseph, the lass was almost dead for the saint's sake. This woman had invaded his being from the moment he laid eyes on her eight long months ago and now she lay with him. God in Heaven, what ye be doin' to me?

Even the time spent with his lovely Amethyst at the Social Club, he'd seen this woman's face. She called for Walker, who must be her husband, and he didn't *faigh muin* married women, though his manly desire failed to acknowledge the missive.

He spooned his body around her. His erection caused him physical pain as her arse rested against him. Another wave of shudders raked through her body, and she shook in torrents. Callum embraced her, bidding the shaking to stop, her welfare more important than his urges. Her torso shook, then stopped and started again until her teeth chattered together. He kissed the top of her head. "I've got ye. *Noo jist haud on.*" And he held her in his arms until the trembles stopped and her breaths steadied.

The fire burned low; the room cooled from the wind that penetrated the crevasses of the structure. Callum placed logs on the hearth and stoked the flames. He glanced at the clock on the wall. Two in the morning. It was three in the afternoon when they'd arrived. He tiptoed over the wood floor to the kitchen and built a fire in the wood stove in case she woke and needed sustenance.

The Scotsman hurried back to the warmth of the makeshift bed, lay beside the woman, and held her close. She rested her head on his shoulder and put her leg over his. His arm held her snugly. Secure in the knowledge she would live, he let himself drift to sleep.

A yelp and the draft of cold air as the blanket was yanked from his body woke him. He rubbed his eyes and focused on the red-haired lady standing over him.

"Where are my clothes?" She raked her eyes over his body, her breath caught, and she covered her mouth with her hand to stifle a scream. "Did you, did we? Who are you?" She grabbed the fireplace poker and raised it over her head. "I asked you a question and I want answers right now or I'll…"

The sight of the woman, her attempt to cover her body with the blanket, and the poker poised over her head caused a chuckle. He quelled the urge to laugh and jumped to stand, naked except for the pillow he used to hide what appeared to be his permanent erection for life. "I rescued you from the blizzard. You and your horse were almost frozen to death. I had no other way of warming you than with my body heat." Callum disguised his laughter with a clearing of his throat as the lady held the blanket on her back while she stepped into her bloomers.

The blanket fell to the floor, and she continued her rant. "You are no gentleman. It's not polite to watch a lady dress." She faced him and fastened her buttons. "Amused, are you?"

He threw the pillow to the settee. He gazed around the room at their predicament and let his laughter loose. She joined him as raucous guffaws filled every crook and cranny.

The amusement died down as she raked her eyes over his body. "A respectable gentleman would put on his clothes."

He grabbed his pants, yanked them on, and stuffed

his semi-hard manhood inside. He buttoned his pants and tugged on his shirt. "Aye, lass ye be right. Me name is Callum MacPhilip. I happened upon ye yesterday on Old Cheyenne Road. I rescued you and your horse. I didn't molest ye, just had to warm your body or you would have died."

She extended her hand. "I'm much obliged."

Instead of a handshake, he kissed the back of her outreached hand. "And what is your name, lass?"

She gazed into his eyes. "You may call me 'Songbird'." She grasped his arm and whispered. "Daisy, my horse. Is she?"

Callum tucked his shirt in his pants and pulled on his boots. "Ah, *dinnae ken*. The mare is in the barn. I'll check on her."

She grabbed her cape. "I'm coming with you."

He placed a blanket around her shoulders and guided her to the settee. "No, lass. You aren't recovered enough to brave the cold. I'll check on Daisy. Won't take long."

He crossed the room while his mind raced in a dozen directions and prayed her horse was still alive.

A woman alone on the road to Wylder, Wyoming roused his suspicions. An apprehensive reality niggled into his brain and caused him to worry for the redhead's safety. Songbird was not a name; it was a nickname.

Time would tell her true identity and who she was running from. His suede coat rested on a peg beside the front door. He tugged it on and grabbed his hat, tipping it to the lady. The trek to the barn was difficult through the banks of snow. Footprints led from the big house to the barn and around to the chicken coop.

The horses had been fed and cared for as expected.

He entered the barn; Daisy stuck her head out of a stall next to Icefall. Both horses munched on fresh hay. Their bottom jaws chomped in a sideways motion. They presented him with a curious stare and went back to their breakfast.

"Daisy, me lass. How'd ye fare?" He examined the mare from nose to tail and found no signs of frost bite. His blood ran cold at the thought he could have found Songbird and the horse days later, both dead from hypothermia.

A check on Duchess found the reddish-brown Clydesdale mare at rest in her stall. She'd have her foal in a few months and Icefall would be the proud father. The first in what he hoped would be a successful endeavor into the breeding of draft horses.

He left the barn and gazed at the blue sky spotted with white clouds. The snow had ceased but it was cold, and the wind blew the snow from the roof of the barn to the ground making deep snowdrifts. They always had an early spring snowstorm or two, but this one arrived unexpected and heavy. He stopped by the hen house and gathered a few eggs for breakfast.

Callum entered his house and found the girl in the rocking chair sipping a cup of coffee. Damn, she was a sight he'd love to see every time he entered his dwelling. "Yer horse be fine. Left her warm and happy munching hay in the stable."

She rested her head on the back of the chair, closed her eyes, and raised her head toward the ceiling. "Thank you, sweet Mother Mary."

"God watched out for the two of you and sent me to your rescue." He sauntered to the kitchen and poured himself a cup of coffee. The pondering question he'd lived with since he found them was why had God brought the deepest desire of his heart to tempt him? A curse or a blessing? Time would tell.

"Hungry?" he asked as he shuffled into the sitting room.

"Yes. Mr. MacPhilip. I hope you don't mind that I made coffee." She stood from the chair and steadied herself.

"Please call me Callum. No need to be formal." He placed the cup on the side table and guided her to the kitchen. "I'm preparing breakfast with fresh eggs from the chickens. You sit here and drink your coffee." A small blanket rested on the back of a straight chair, and he placed it over her legs.

He mixed biscuits in a bowl with his hands, patted them in a pan, and placed them in the hot stove. Pieces of salted pork fatback were nestled in a skillet and set on the hot eye. The meat sizzled while the biscuits baked. Callum glanced at the lady as he cooked. She was the first woman to grace his home and she looked right sitting in his kitchen. As right as rain on a spring day in May. He hummed while he cracked eggs into a bowl and whipped them with a fork to scramble in the grease.

After a quick set of the table with plates, silverware, butter, and the boysenberry jam bought on the last trip to Cheyenne, breakfast was ready for his guest. He walked to her chair, helped her stand, and assisted her to the table. "Breakfast is served, me lady." With the blanket folded and secured around her shoulders, she straightened her spine and sat regally before him. The lass put on a good front but couldn't hide the fact she was weak as a newborn foal.

"Hope ye like me cooking." He retrieved his cup from the front room and grabbed the coffee pot and refilled both cups.

She held onto the blanket as if it was her lifeline. "This smells wonderful. Never met a man who could cook." She placed a biscuit on her plate.

He spooned jelly from the jar. "The jam is boysenberry, reminds me of the spread me ma would make." The eggs and pork were placed before her before any food touched his plate.

"You're Scottish," she said with confidence.

"And ye be Irish. Would know from the red locks of hair and the slight accent." He hesitated then continued. "Ye called out for Walker during yer sleep." She stared, her gaze cold as the ice outside. "I'm sorry, lass, didn't mean to be nosy." He drank a sip of coffee and glanced her way. "Don't want your man to think I did anything but rescue you. Don't need a jealous husband calling for a lynch mob, ye *ken*?"

"I'm not married." She stared at the plate and scooped eggs on her fork.

He'd let the subject drop for now, but he'd find out who this Walker was before she left to go wherever it was she was headed. "Soon as the weather breaks, I'll see to yer carriage."

Her fork clinked against the plate as it fell from her grasp. "I forgot about my buggy. It holds everything I own." She stood and almost tipped over her chair.

He grabbed her arm. "No one's going to bother it. I'll see to it as soon as the snow starts to melt."

She eased back in her seat, hands in her lap. "Thank you, Callum." Their eyes met and her lips lifted in a slight smile.

He studied her. Aye, she be running from someone. Callum gathered their dishes and placed them in the sink.

She picked up a cloth. "Allow me to help."

He placed a chair close to the sink. "Sit and talk to me while I work." He tucked the blanket around her legs. His hand lingered on her thigh before he returned his attention to his chore.

****

The Scotsman washed and dried the dishes with ease and confidence and placed the dishware on the shelves with care. She'd never had a man cook for her much less seen one wash a dirty dish. Hold onto your heart. He needed a woman who could give him a family, not a barren nothing of a woman like herself. As soon as the road was passable, she'd start her new life in Wylder. "How long have you been in the states? With your brogue, I assume you were born in Scotland."

"Aye, ye be correct." He dried the forks and placed them with the others on the shelf. "By your Irish lilt, I expect you to be born in Ireland?"

"Yes." She nodded. "My family sailed to New York when I was seven."

"Why Wyoming?" He opened the firebox on the wood stove to let the heat fill the room.

"Eleven years past, we were on our way to California, but my Papa fell in love with the Wyoming countryside, and we settled in Cheyenne. They both caught the fever a year after we arrived and died two days apart." She stared at the floor remembering the events like it was yesterday.

He knelt in front of her chair and enfolded her hand

in his. "I'm so sorry, lass. So much pain for a young lady."

She cradled the sides of his head in her hands. His curly reddish-brown hair fell below his ears and his well-trimmed beard suited his handsome face. An urge to kiss him swept over her. As if he read her mind, he lifted her from the chair and brushed a kiss across her lips. She melted into his embrace and rested her head on his chest. His body was hard as molded steel, and his muscles rippled as he enfolded her in a tender embrace. She'd never been this protected and cared for in her thirty years of life.

He put his hand under her chin and lifted her face. His lips were on hers before she could speak. Searching. Probing. Demanding. A man, a woman each lost in the intensity of desire. The image of him naked made her core lust after a connection. She let herself feel for the first time in years, feel the affection, feel the lust, feel the love. When the kiss was over, her body instinctively gravitated toward him desiring more.

"Come." He steadied her with his arm around her waist and guided her to his bedroom. "I want you to rest, comfortable in a bed, not on the floor."

They entered a bright room with a large ornately carved bed, dressing table and mirror, and large wardrobe. The Scotsman appeared to be a strong, rough cowboy, but she was learning he was more refined and intelligent than Walker. How could she compare a devil to Callum MacPhilip? With this new start, she hoped to forget about the past, but it would take a lifetime to rid herself of Walker Morgan.

He placed her in a chair, removed her boots, and helped her undress down to her chemise and bloomers.

"I'll be in the next room. Call out of ye need anything."

He tucked the quilts around her, placed a kiss on her forehead, and smoothed her hair. Her gaze followed him as he put another log in the fireplace and stoked the fire. At the recognition of him this morning after she'd willed herself to stop staring at his magnificent body and focus on his face, she'd sent a thank you prayer to St. Jude, the saint of hopeless cases. Callum was no stranger, she'd seen him a few times in Cheyenne. Once when Walker escorted her to a special gala where she would perform, she spotted him across the street. As her eyes locked with those of the ruggedly handsome man, she warred with herself to run to the stranger. To leave Walker was hard; he's all she'd known since her parents died. He'd refused to marry her and when she discovered the kind of person he was, she was grateful. If circumstances were different, she'd allow herself to love this kind man.

Her body melted into the comfortable feather bed and the heavy quilts warmed her still cold feet. Callum's scent of leather, lavender, and hay lingered on the pillow. She inhaled a deep breath and let sleep take her.

Chapter Two

Callum eased into the bedroom, stood over the bed, and listened as the lass breathed. The assurance she would recover raked over him like the heat from the fireplace that flickered a few feet away. She lay on her side with her hair billowing behind her. Her pale skin spotted with a few faint freckles made him want to touch her. He'd cared for many women and respected them, even the whores. But love. The day his eyes beheld her in Cheyenne, it was as if Cupid's arrow entered his head right between his eyes and burrowed love into his brain and heart. He inhaled a deep breath and let it out slow and quiet wanting to stay and watch her instead of getting to the ranch tasks.

He donned his coat and hat and ventured out in the early afternoon assessing the work to be done as soon as the weather improved. Water wept from the icicles along the top of the house to produce a ping, ping, ping as they dripped on the porch and ground.

The horse herd shuffled through the melting snow in the pasture, already adjusted to the freak snowstorm after the teasing taste of spring a few weeks before. They recognized as he did soon the earth would warm and ready itself for a new season. The chickens remained close to their roost, but the pigs had already made their snow-covered pens into a muddy mess. He assured himself the animals were well fed and cared for before he made his way to Daniel's home.

Sarah greeted him. "Come inside, you'll catch your death."

He dusted the snow off his boots and paused before he entered. "I can take my shoes off."

"No need. Daniel's in the study and there's a roaring fire. Go in and I'll serve hot tea. Made scones this morning." She gave him a devious smile.

"My recipe?" He placed his coat on the hall tree.

She plodded to the kitchen. "Of course, and I added raisins."

"Sounds like a bribe to me." He chuckled as he headed toward the study.

Daniel sat at his desk writing a missive. "Red, come in, have a seat. How's the stock?"

"They be fine." Callum sat in a chair in front of the desk. "How's the paperwork?"

"Tedious." Daniel folded the letter and placed it in an envelope.

"That's why it takes an educated lawyer to run the business side. You're the brains and I'm the muscle." He glanced around the large room and ideas of enlarging his house filled his mind.

"Nonsense." Daniel placed a ledger on his desk. "Since you're here, need for you to study over fourth-quarter figures. We had the best year since we started the ranch." He passed the book to his partner.

The Scotsman studied the calculations. "Wait till we get the Clydesdale side going. You'll see another increase."

Sarah entered the room with a tray and Daniel jumped from his desk. "Allow me. You shouldn't be lifting anything heavy."

"I'm with child, not an invalid." Sarah sat on the settee. "Come, take a break, and have some tea and scones."

The men passed a perceptive grin between them before they sat, Daniel beside his wife and Red in the nearest chair.

Sarah poured tea in her porcelain cups and passed scones. "Now, Callum what is this I hear about you rescuing a damsel in distress?" She tilted her head and glanced over her teacup before taking a sip.

The Scotsman ate half his scone and sipped the tea before responding. "I think you're a better scone maker than me." He leaned toward the platter to retrieve more sweet bread.

Sarah slapped his hand. "Not until you tell me about your visitor. Who is she? Where was she headed? Is she well?"

"Her name is Songbird. Ah *dinnae ken* the reason for her to be on Old Cheyenne Road, but seems she was headed to Wylder from Cheyenne. She and her horse were near frozen to death when I happened upon them. Seems to be recovering, I checked on her throughout the day and she's sleeping." He took a chance and chose two scones from the plate.

"Is there a Mr. Songbird?" Daniel ventured to ask.

"No, says she isn't married." Callum poured tea into his cup and refilled his host's cups. "I know you two are thinking the same thing I am. The reason a person won't tell their real name is they're in hiding from someone." He stared at them and waited for their nod to continue. "Daniel, do you remember last year when we traveled to the sale in Cheyenne?"

"Yes, you bought Icefall and I purchased a quarter

horse." He stoked the fire.

"Remember the redhead who got in the carriage with the older man?" He gazed up at Daniel and their eyes met.

Daniel stared and tilted his head. "She is the woman you now have in your house?"

"Aye." Callum strolled to the window. He stared into the snow-covered distance. "God is either punishing me for not going to confession in six years or he's rewarding me for something. Ah *dinnae ken* how it will work out."

Sarah motioned for the men to sit. "If you ever want raisin scones again, Callum MacPhilip, you better tell me about this mysterious lady."

Daniel sat and held his wife's hand, but Red stood. "An angel of a woman caught my eye as she boarded a carriage. She was dressed in finery like you wore when you arrived in Wylder. The lass' red hair curled down her back in waves. She was the most beautiful vision of loveliness I'd ever seen. I searched the streets for the lady every time I passed through Cheyenne. Imagine my surprise when I got her to me house and discovered she was the same woman."

"Have you told her?" Daniel adjusted a pillow behind his wife's back.

"Daniel, don't fuss so." Sarah squirmed on the sofa.

"Not sure if I'll mention the encounter. I'm sure she doesn't remember me." Callum smiled at the two. So much in love and so devoted to each other. Daniel found his match. "As much as I'd like to stay and watch you two love birds fawn over each other, I need to check on the lass."

Sarah wobbled toward the door. "I made stew to share with you. Grab your coat and go through the kitchen."

He meandered to the back of the house followed by Daniel. "Miss Sarah, you should'na gone to any trouble."

Sarah presented him with a lard pail full of stew. "No trouble, we all have to eat. When Songbird is well enough, I want to meet her."

Callum let out a puff of air and exchanged a grin with Daniel, both certain the lady wouldn't get off this property until Sarah found out everything there was to know about her.

He eased inside the back door and left the tin bucket on the table and removed his boots. He roamed through the house in sock feet and peeked in the bedroom. Rose's gentle snore echoed through the room.

The chair creaked when he sat, and she snuggled further into the quilt. Her hair spilled over the pillow and her beautiful face relaxed into a peaceful sleep. The vision of her in his bed tugged at his heart as strong as it had the moment he met her gaze in Cheyenne. She was the first who had heated his blood with a single glance. The act of mating he was well acquainted with and by the age of her, he was certain she'd had her share of men. His desire, ready for the act, had him anxious to crawl in the bed and take her, but his heart bade him wait.

The closest he'd come to making love was with Amethyst. The prostitute had been his Saturday night since he'd arrived in Wylder from Kentucky. She was a beautiful dark-haired vixen with womanly curves and a tiger in the bedroom. He'd even considered taking her for a wife, but now a certain nameless redhead redirected his thoughts and his heart in a new direction. A prayer escaped his lips. "God, give me the strength to let her go if must needs."

****

Rose woke to light streaming through the curtains and raced to the water closet. She tiptoed back in the room and stared in the wall mirror over the dresser and smoothed her tousled hair. She tugged the wrinkled dress over her head and glanced in the mirror as she fastened the buttons. Callum stood at the entrance. "What time is it?" she asked.

He stepped into the room. "It's eight in the morn."

She didn't understand. The last she remembered it was Sunday morning and Callum tucked her in bed. "How long did I sleep?"

"Near twenty-four hours, lass. Aye, the rest did ye good." He approached and placed his hands on her shoulders.

Rose surrendered and let him enfold his arms around her as his scent invaded her nostrils. The protective feel of his arms along with his warmth drugged her, making her hold tight, his touch a calming balm to her shattered soul. He stepped away and the absence of his touch pained her. She disregarded the attraction as if it was an old dish rag. She wouldn't, she couldn't hurt this man and if he fell in love with her, she would.

He led her to the kitchen. "I've cooked breakfast for you, and after you eat, I'll prepare a nice warm bath." She sat and allowed him to scoot her chair close to the table. "Prepared me special scones with clotted cream."

19

He poured coffee in a thick white mug and fixed her a plate of the delicate bread.

"You cooked scones?" She glanced from the food to his face. A slight frown graced his forehead as if she'd offended him. "I've never known a man talented at so many things." The memory of his naked body ready for action had her core melting with the knowledge he'd be talented at that also.

He sat in the chair across from her. "Go on, then. How do you like them?"

She broke off a piece of scone and slathered it with cream. The flaky bread melted in her mouth. "Delicious. Reminds me of my ma's. You are the most amazing man." She devoured several more of the small confections. "How's the weather?" She drank the last sip of her coffee.

He filled the sink with their dishes. "Ice is melting from the roof, temperature warming. I expect Daniel and I can get your carriage to you by Wednesday."

"Daniel?" Not knowing where they were, she assumed no one lived on the land.

"My partner in the ranch. Daniel started the horse ranch and I worked for him 'til last year when he married Sarah Miller and made me a partner. Daniel joked he got married twice in one month." He busied himself with the dishes.

Rose grabbed a cloth and dried. "Do they live close?"

"Aye. Soon as the snow melts, I'll show you around. Sarah wants to meet you."

She placed the plate on the shelf and let out a slow breath. "They know I'm here?" If gossip got out about her staying with Callum she'd be labeled as a loose woman. Why would that matter after the way she'd lived the last ten years? Most of the people in Cheyenne treated her and Walker as if they were married, but she'd lived in sin and now paid the penance for her immorality. Intimacy with one other besides Walker with the intention to make him jealous and stop cheating on her had backfired. He had his men almost beat the man to death. People ignored men who had illicit liaisons while a woman was branded a whore.

He put his hands on her shoulders. "Don't worry, lass. They're my family. No gossip will leave this property. You're safe, I promise." Callum lifted the kettle of hot water and poured it into the tub. "Don't have any fancy soap or oils, but you'll be clean. Wish I could get your trunk. I know how ladies want to change dresses. I'll hang your clothes in front of the fire to freshen them while you bathe."

He placed a rag, soap, and large cloth on a chair beside the tub, then turned his back. "Go on, then. Take off yer clothes and climb in the tub. I won't watch."

She folded her arms across her chest and stared at his back and debated whether to trust him. Even if he did watch her undress, he'd seen her naked, and a faint remembrance of his long body stretched out with hers nibbled at the pleasure point of her brain. Rose hurried out of her clothes and stepped into the tub before he changed his mind and decided to watch. The allure of the warm bath elicited a sigh from her lips as the water spilled over her. "Thank you." Rose closed her eyes and let out a breath, one she'd held in her chest since resigning herself to death in the storm. Settled into the warm bath, her eyes wandered around the room. The Scotsman was true to his word, he'd let her be.

"The Braes of Balquhidder" tore through her heart like a lance. Callum sang the song in a soft baritone. His voice, pure and clear, drifted from the front room. Tears welled in her eyes at the strains of the first song her father taught her. It was said she was blessed in inheriting his talent, but his Irish tenor always outperformed her mezzo-soprano. How many times had she sung the harmony with her pa? If the snow had taken her, she'd be with them now. Reunited in heaven, if God let her in after how she'd lived since her ma and pa had departed this life. The water drew her under until her thirst for air made her splash to the surface.

The Scotsman appeared as if by magic. "Ye be all right, lass?"

Rose shook her head and let the water splash from her hair. "Yes." She rubbed the bar of soap along her scalp. The smell of lavender reminded her of Callum's pillow. She immersed her head to remove the soap. When she opened her eyes, the Scotsman leaned against the wall. His gaze was a magnet. She couldn't breathe, didn't want to.

"*Tà tù iontach àlainn.*" He knelt beside the tub and washed her neck and back with the cloth. "Aye, me Songbird, ye be such a beautiful lass." He guided her head underwater to wash away the remainder of the soap.

She gasped for air and swallowed at the same time; her reflexes returned to normal with his touch. He helped her stand, the water sloshed from the metal tub to the floor. She placed her hand in his and held onto his shoulder with the other, stepping out of the tub. He dried her body with the towel and scooped her in his arms. He held her close, his suede vest stiff against her skin while a button dug into her side. She experienced the deprivation as soon as he released her onto the bed, the connection lost.

Callum undressed and didn't hesitate to join her. The bed sank as his body invaded the mattress. "I need to *ken* ye." he whispered.

The powerful kiss he gave her stole her heart. She cursed herself for doing this, but she couldn't stop. His hands were everywhere, on her breast teasing her nipples and between her legs exploring. He inserted two fingers inside her.

"Ye be ready for me." He kissed his way from her neck to her breast and sucked the tender bud.

The connection from her breast to her core created a longing she'd never experienced. Walker had taken her for his pleasure only. This man was magic. The gentle touch of his fingers on her skin, the tender way he held her in his strong arms, the attention he gave to every inch of her body. Could she have died and gone to heaven? She opened her eyes and raked her hands through his tousled hair as he explored. Soft moans escaped his throat as he took his time loving every inch of her body with his gentle caresses. Her hips moved wanting more, wanting him. "Take me, Callum."

"Aye, I'll take ye, lass." He teased her nipple with his tongue. "I'm gonna please ye first."

He placed his hand on her mound to steady her, sucked her peaks with his mouth and did the most wonderful things with his fingers inside her. She rocked against his hand ready to explode. "Callum." She whispered as the wave lifted her until the sense of weightlessness made her cry out. "Please, Callum." She climbed higher and higher as if she floated in the air. A soft cry escaped her lips. "Love me." The spasm started, she clutched his hair and called his name as if it were a sacred prayer. He continued pleasing her until her body stilled. She spread her legs and tugged his hard body toward her. Her mind screamed this was wrong, but her heart would break if she didn't have him. His gaze burned into her eyes as he performed the act of giving and taking. Giving pleasure, taking pleasure, giving a heart, taking a heart. She held onto his strong arms watching as a man loved her as no other ever had before.

He called as his love spilled inside her. "*Tà mo chroi istigh ionat.*" My heart is in you.

He kept his large body above her and kissed her mouth, his tongue searching. He rolled to his back and held her to his side.

He wiped a tear from her face. "Ye all right?"

"Yes." No. She'd never be fine, never again. The pain of wanting something so desperately and not being able to have it never left her. She resigned herself and memorized each moment experienced in this safe house with this gentle giant. This memory along with the money she earned in Wylder would help her on her quest to a new life in California.

Chapter Three

The sun beamed on the earth and melted the snow drifts while birds sat on tree limbs. Their morning song welcomed the cold spring day. Callum stepped over the chickens who'd ventured out of their pen and pecked at grass that peeked above the melting snow. He performed the morning chores while memories of his time spent with Songbird never left his brain. He told her he loved her. Words he'd never said to another except for his dear departed *Mathair.* The words tumbled out of his mouth. At least they were in Gaelic. Maybe she didn't recognize the endearment. He worked the ranch, milked the cow, checked the herd, and gazed at his house with the knowledge that she rested there. His life changed the moment she cried out his name as he loved her. She'd been on his mind for months, and now she had infiltrated his heart.

Callum knocked on Daniel's kitchen door and called out. "Fresh milk, Miss Sarah."

Sarah wore a plain dress with an apron that covered her growing belly. "Thank you. I need milk; I'm making a cake this morning."

He set the pail on the table. "Fresh milk it is."

She dipped a cup in the warm cow's milk. "Daniel's in the study if you need to see him. How's your Songbird?" She bit her lip and tried not to smile.

The smirk didn't go unnoticed, and his face

reddened. "She be getting stronger."

Sarah giggled. "I want to meet her before she leaves this ranch."

"Aye." He left the kitchen and headed to the sitting room.

Daniel dipped his pen in the inkwell and signed a paper. "Last of the signing. I'm ready to go to work." He placed his pen in its porcelain holder and gazed up at his friend. "You look like horse shit."

Callum put his hands on his hips and glared. "I be fine, working in the cold is all."

Daniel stood and placed his hands on the desk. "You are sick, but I don't believe it's physical." He dashed around the desk and faced his friend. "You bedded her, didn't you?"

"And if I did?" He straightened. "We're adults. You had Sarah before you married her."

Daniel put his hands in front of him. "I'm not casting a stone, just pray this works out for you. Heaven knows you need a woman in your life before you catch something from The Social Club."

His friend was sincere. Daniel was the closest to a brother he'd ever known. "Hold yer blathering, we've work to do."

Daniel grabbed his coat. "What can I help with?"

"We need to see to the lass's carriage." They ambled to the barn to saddle the horses. "Snows melting and Icefall should have no trouble towing the buggy to the ranch."

****

Rose busied herself with sweeping the floor and tidying up the hearth where the fire had raged since she arrived. Soot and dust were swept away with the broom as she studied the Scotsman's home. Everything reflected him. Heavy cast-iron replicas of horses were scattered along the thick wooden mantel. The rugs were bright and colorful, and the black leather settee held the permanent indention where he sat.

The front door swung open, and Callum entered with her trunk. "Daniel and I were able to get the buggy. Snow's melting and we can get you to Wylder in the morn. I imagine that's where you were headed."

"Yes, I have a job waiting for me." She opened her trunk to check her belongings. "The carriage wasn't disturbed?"

"The snowbanks had the wheels trapped, but Icefall hauled it out." He hung his coat on the wall peg.

"Must be a strong horse." She found her blue dress and examined it.

Callum warmed his hands by the fire. "My draft horse. He's a Clydesdale."

Rose stepped to the bedroom. "Thank you, I'm happy to have a clean dress to wear."

She smoothed the material of the blue skirt as she entered the sitting room.

He turned his back toward the hearth. "What kind of job do ye have in Wylder?"

"I'm a singer." She raked her eyes along his tall body.

"Aye, had that much figured with your name being Songbird and all. Is Song yer first name and Bird yer last? He crossed his arms over his chest and glared. "And where will ye be singing?"

"The Five Star Saloon. Boone Layton's a friend. You know him?" she answered, somehow wanting his approval but knowing he wouldn't give it.

"Boone's a friend and a finer piano player I've never known." He stared at her pretty, clean dress. "How do you know Boone?"

She led him to the settee and sat. He lowered his tall frame beside her, the cushions sank, and her body gravitated close to his. "You've been kind to me, and you've asked nothing about my past although I'm sure you're curious."

"I am." He searched her face for more answers.

His scrutiny caused heat to flush her cheeks. She stared at the flames and reflected on her life in Cheyenne.

He rested his hand on her arm. "If it's too painful, lass, you don't have to tell me."

She gazed at her lap. His large hand caressed hers with tenderness. "My name is Rose O'Brien. I was a singer and actress at The Cheyenne City Opera House. Boone was the accompanist and directed a few performances. Walker Morgan owns the theater. I lived with him for ten years. We were lovers. He's not a kind man, and Boone stood up for me on more than one occasion. Walker fired him."

"Did Mr. Morgan hit you?" Callum's voice was soft, but his face held a grimace and his jaw twitched as he ground his teeth.

"Yes." Ashamed to admit how many times, she continued. "One time, Boone confronted him, punched Walker, and knocked him out. When he came to, he sent for the sheriff. Boone was escorted out of town."

"And you didn't tell the sheriff the truth?" He lifted her chin.

"We tried. Who do you think he believed? A woman and a Negro man or a fine upstanding business owner? Walker can buy his way out of anything." Her heart hurt from the disappointment that glimmered from his eyes.

"Boone's been in Wylder for almost two years. That means you stayed in Cheyenne with Walker." He released her hand and lifted her chin searching her eyes for an answer.

"It's complicated, Callum. I don't expect you to understand. It took a while for me to get my fill of his cheating, lying, and affairs. I had no family, no one to run to. Singing is all I know, and until I save enough money to go to California or Oregon, I have no other choice." She put her hand on his cheek. "I don't want Walker to know where I am, so I will be known in Wylder as Songbird."

"Where will you live?" He added more wood to the fire and stoked the flames.

"Culpepper's Boarding House." She stood beside him and warmed her hands. "I'm a grown woman capable of making decisions."

His eyes raked over her body. "I *ken* ye are."

"Why do I feel like a little girl asking her father's permission?" She waited for his answer.

"Have you ever been to Wylder?"

"No." She folded her hands across her chest.

"As Daniel always says, they don't call it Wylder, Wyoming for nothing." He meandered to the door. "Get your cloak—Sarah wants to meet you." Callum placed the hood of her cape over her head and guided her to the front porch. "Sarah and Daniel can be trusted."

They waited on the front porch of Sarah's home. The trek through the soggy earth had been difficult in her leather boots. The Scotsman had lifted her in his arms twice to carry her over mud holes. She checked the bottom of her shoes for mud and found none. The door opened and she gazed into the eyes of a petite woman with a protruding belly. A tired sadness roiled in her stomach as it did when reminded of her inability to bear a child.

Sarah stepped on the porch. "You must be Songbird."

Rose found herself engulfed in a hug. The young lady led her into the house. "My name is Rose O'Brien, and it's nice to meet you, Sarah. Callum speaks highly of you and Daniel."

The lady of the house addressed Callum. "Are you visiting with us?"

The Scotsman shook his head. "No, I believe you ladies need to have your tea and talk. I'll check out Old Cheyenne Road and make sure it's safe for travel tomorrow."

Sarah led her visitor to the front room. "I'm so happy to have another female to talk to. This is my first winter in Wyoming, and I miss Laurel, Leona, and Mary. I even miss my Aunt Mildred."

Rose sat on the end of the settee while Sarah lounged in a large chair. "How far along are you?"

She rested her hand on her belly. "Seven months." Sarah laughed. "Give me your hand."

Rose extended her hand and Sarah placed it on her belly. She'd never touched another woman's body, but Sarah was so excited about the new life growing inside her, Rose did as she was commanded. A movement under her hand caused her to jerk away. "What was that?"

"The baby is strong; it kicks and moves at the

oddest times. Wakes me up at night. I think it'll be a night owl." She rubbed her swollen stomach.

"I haven't been around many soon-to-be mothers." Sarah's excitement and innocence caused her to care for this new friend and forget about her inadequacies.

"How old are you?" Sarah asked.

The young woman's question took her aback. "I'm thirty." Since they were talking age, she asked. "And you?"

"I'll be twenty-two this year, and Daniel is six years my senior." A slight smile crossed her lips. "Callum will be thirty-six come July. Same age difference for the both of you."

"We aren't a couple." Rose inhaled a breath and raised her head. This young lady was trying to play matchmaker and she'd have none of it.

Sarah gave her a huge smile. "Callum is the best person I know, except for my Daniel. You could do a lot worse." She smiled an insightful grin. "I don't mean to pry."

Rose apologized. "I'm sorry. I'm determined to start a new life for myself, and I don't need the burden of a handsome Scotsman weighing me down."

Sarah stretched and rubbed her back. "I'm happy to hear you admit he's handsome. I was worried you had a problem with your eyesight." She stood. "I made a vanilla cake this morning. I need help with the tray if you don't mind. Promised my husband I wouldn't lift anything heavy until after the babe comes."

She followed her friend into the kitchen and studied the beautiful furnishings. "Didn't expect to see such a fine dwelling on a horse ranch."

"Daniel used his parents' home in Kentucky as a

model for this one. He says their house is twice this size." She poured hot water into a teapot. "I told him this one is big enough for us. Any bigger and I'd spend all my time cleaning."

They settled into the gossip of new fashions and Sarah advised her to be extra careful living in Wylder. She agreed to meet Sarah and her friends for tea as soon as the weather permitted. Having friends was a foreign concept. Walker had controlled her life and career claiming she had no time for frivolity.

****

Callum placed his rifle in the saddle scabbard and directed Icefall toward Wylder, examining the road along the way. The horse trotted to the Five Star Saloon without guidance and stopped at the hitching post. With the stallion secured, he grabbed his rifle and stalked into the saloon.

He sat at a table and glared out the window.

Sonny Cash addressed him. "Whiskey?"

"Aye." He situated his rifle against the wall. "Boone here?"

Sonny approached with the whiskey bottle and glass. "In the back."

"Need to talk to the both of ye." Callum downed a shot of whiskey and poured another.

The piano player and bartender approached the table and sat.

Boone Layton placed a glass on the table and poured a drink. "What's on your mind?"

His gaze settled on the men. "Rose O'Brien." He leaned back in his chair and studied their reactions.

Layton was the first to speak. "Is she all right? I swear if Walker Morgan found out she was runnin' and hurt her, I'll kill him myself."

"How do you know Rose?" Sonny asked.

He drank another shot and pounded the table with the glass. "She be fine and she's an acquaintance. I'm here to tell ye if any man in this saloon touches a hair on her red head, they will answer to me. Spread the word."

Sonny laughed. "Never met her in person, but Boone says she's thirty and that's too young for me."

"I like my women dark and sweet." Layton poured another shot of drink.

"Tell me about Morgan." Callum stared at Boone.

"The man's a snake. Dishonest. Liar. Cheat. You name it. Don't know why a fine lady such as Rose wasted years of her young life with the likes of him. You won't see him get his hands dirty. He pays men to do his nasty jobs." He crossed his arms on the table. "You're in love with her."

The Scotsman scooted his chair away and stood. "No, don't like to see any person bullied, man or woman." He retrieved his rifle. "See to it you spread the word before she starts her job here."

Layton nodded. "I'll watch out best I can." He hesitated. "She doesn't want anyone knowing her real name."

"Aye, Songbird." Callum nodded toward Sonny. "That what you're advertising her as?"

"Yes." Sonny gathered the money from the table along with the bottle and glasses. "And I don't want trouble any more than you."

Callum arrived at the ranch and settled Icefall in his stall. He made his way to collect Rose.

Daniel greeted him. "How's the road?"

He hung his coat on the hall tree. "It'll be safe to travel tomorrow." Female laughter wafted from the sitting room. "They still going at it?"

"All afternoon. And don't think you'll get out of here before supper. Sarah has someone to talk to and they've already planned you'll stay for stew." He accompanied the Scotsman to the kitchen. "Sarah wants you to make biscuits."

Callum donned the white apron resting on a peg and rolled up his sleeves. "Better get to it."

Daniel poured them both a cup of coffee and sat to watch. "Many people out and about?"

He gathered ingredients. "Streets in Wylder are mud. Still some drifts and ice between here and there. Temperature's warming. In a few days, won't be a trace left."

"Where'd you go in town?" Daniel asked more as a statement than a question.

"Why?" He poured milk into the flour and lard mixture.

Daniel lowered his voice. "Heard the women talking. Songbird, I mean Rose, said she's a singer and has a job at the Five Star." He swirled the liquid in his cup. "I'm sure you got it out of her, and if I know you, you visited the saloon and staked your claim."

The Scotsman swallowed his temper. "Needed to make it clear to Cash and Layton I wouldn't accept anyone causing Rose harm. She's been through enough in Cheyenne."

"Yeah, found out about Walker Morgan, too." He refilled his cup.

"What'd you do, sit outside the door and listen?" Callum patted biscuits in the pan.

"I sat on the stairs; they didn't know I was there." He helped his friend wash the dishes.

"Bullocks." Callum let out a loud chuckle. "Miss Sarah knows everything you do. You'll take hades for the eavesdropping when we leave."

Chapter Four

Callum nestled Rose in his arms and carried her from the big house to his smaller one. He opened the door with his right hand and cradled her with the other. They crossed the threshold, and he kicked the door shut with his foot. He'd wanted to kiss her lips through the entire dinner. He found them now and devoured them. Sweeter than the cake Miss Sarah had made. "Uhmm…" He moaned as he tasted her. The hold she had on his neck tightened. Reason over need won and he let her slide to the floor. The room had cooled—the fireplace needed wood. It wouldn't do for her to get a chill.

She stood beside him as he worked and warmed her hands in front of the fire. When the wood blazed, he hung his hat and coat on the peg and stripped her cloak from her. It had been an enjoyable dinner with the Taylors, but the small talk didn't satisfy him, only having Rose again would. This could be their last moments together, as he had no idea how things would play out in Wylder. It was obvious she enjoyed the sex and closeness they'd shared, but the woman held herself aloof as if she had a secret agenda. "Ye be warm enough?" he asked.

"Yes, perfectly fine." She warmed her hands above the flames and turned to heat her back. "I enjoyed my day with Sarah. I haven't had a friend since I lived in

New York. Walker never…" She stopped talking.

He put a finger to her lips to silence her. "I want you to be that girl again. I *ken* you've not been able to be the woman you were meant to be for a while." He placed an errant strand of hair behind her ear and spoke in a soft voice. "I hope I'll be able to assist you."

She backed away and gazed into his eyes and nodded.

He took this as a sign. He claimed her lips in a sensual kiss. She relaxed her mouth and a sigh escaped causing his pants to tighten. Her body melted into his, submissive but unsure as if she'd never been loved. An arsehole like Morgan would take what he wanted giving nothing in return.

She'd know how a fine lady like her deserved to be loved before she left tomorrow. He brushed kisses over the silky skin on her neck and held her, one hand on her back and the other tangled in her long hair wanting to remain like this the rest of his life. The burning desire to be one with her raged. "*Mo ghràdh.*" He led her to the bedroom, sat her in the chair, and removed every obstacle keeping him from her. With all her clothing piled on the chest, he placed her in his large bed and covered her body with a quilt.

Callum undressed; his eyes gazed into hers the entire time. A grin lined his face as Rose stared while he slid his pants and long underwear to the floor. Her mouth opened, she exhaled a breath as if she wanted to say something, only watching him still.

He crawled into bed beside her and drew her close. Her breasts snuggled against his chest. She wasn't petite, but she wasn't tall either. He estimated her to be sixty-six inches to his seventy-six and thin but with the curves of a woman.

Songbird would have the attention of every man in the saloon, and the idea pained him. But tonight, she was his. Callum kissed her and teased her nipple with his thumb. So ripe and ready for tasting. His mouth found the aroused bud while his hand slipped to the warm folds between her thighs, the urge to enter her so strong he had to stop and take a deep breath, determined not to use her like he imagined Walker Morgan had. She deserved more.

Rose squirmed closer. "How can you wait?"

"Because ye be worth waiting for." His lips found hers, and he busied himself exploring her mouth with his tongue, taking time to taste the skin on her neck and run his hands over her entire body. He continued loving her, massaging her secret place, while she panted and moaned his name.

He lifted his body over hers and their eyes locked together. She guided him inside her.

"*Mo gradh.*" He growled in a whisper. Even if she left town tomorrow, she'd always be his love. Their lovemaking started. The act was so right as if he'd known her his whole life, not just a vision he couldn't get out of his mind for the last few months. She closed her eyes and cried with release, the sight so beautiful he almost stopped but the desire too much. Faster, faster, in and out until he fell from the top of the ridge and poured his seed into her womb.

He rolled them to their side, and her head rested on his arm. He'd not loved a woman but bedded many, Amethyst for the last few years, which fine and dandy until the day Rose caught his eye in Cheyenne. Didn't know her, didn't know if he'd ever see her again, didn't know how to find her, but his heart did. Here she was and he'd be damned if he'd let her go easy.

He drifted to sleep with Rose snuggled on his shoulder, the fear of leaving her in Wylder heavy in his dreams.

"Good morn, *mo gradh*." He tugged her on top of him and filled her center with one stroke. "Do ye know how to ride a horse?"

"I do." She grinned. "I'm an expert horsewoman."

He couldn't take his eyes from her as she pleasured them. Deep breaths and then a moan escaped from somewhere deep inside her. He followed; his hips rose and fell with her rhythm. She collapsed on top of him, and he held her close. The feel of her breasts on his chest and her long mane trailing down his sides he'd not soon forget. The last few days he'd not soon forget either. The fear of her living in Wylder alone made his erection go limp.

She stepped from the bed, and without the warmth of her body the cold air touched his skin. As Rose dressed, he strutted into the front room naked and made a fire. Her comfort was more important than his.

She entered the room and handed him his pants and shirt. "Put these on or you catch your death of cold."

He took his clothes but not before she scanned his body with her eyes. "Like what you see, do ye?"

"I like what I see, very much." She fastened the buttons on his shirt.

Rose retrieved his socks and boots and waited while he fastened the buttons on his pants. "Sit in the chair."

He sat and attempted to take his socks from her,

but she had other ideas. To his amazement, and after several tries, she had his socks on his feet and attempted to get a foot into a boot. She tugged at the leather. Rose fell back on her arse, and he let out a loud laugh. "I appreciate your help, but ye'll not be able to get these on my feet." He pulled on the boots, stood, and helped her to stand. "Never had a woman dress me. I could get used to it."

****

Rose sat in her black buggy holding the reins tight as she steered Daisy down Old Cheyenne Road toward Wylder. The sun warmed the morning, and birds sang and darted from one tree limb to another. The horse's hoofs clomped in the mud and her carriage wheels spun in the few patches of ice and snow. Callum rode ahead atop the largest horse she'd ever seen. The animal was as calm and welcoming as he. She'd stared amazed at how he mounted the giant stallion this morning and how Daisy followed like a lamb. They were a commanding pair.

Fear of being alone in Wylder made her reluctant to leave the ranch, but she couldn't stay there. The Scotsman had been kind, kinder than anyone she'd known, but Walker Morgan had been kind at the start. Pain pricked at her heart as he'd loaded her trunk into the carriage and his eyes had found hers and held them hostage for a moment.

After Callum rescued her, she lived free from danger for the first time since she lost her family, eleven years ago. Peace for a few short days, but it was a start. The Scotsman talked of danger in Wylder, but it couldn't begin to compare with the hell of living in Cheyenne with Walker. As he aged, he became meaner, and the last beating took two weeks for the bruise on her face to disappear. She planned her escape, deciding one day and leaving the next. He'd gone on a trip to Denver. When he returned at the end of this week, she and Daisy would be gone. She bought the carriage and left no trace, told no one of her plans except the telegram she'd sent Boone.

The Scotsman was another matter altogether. What must he think of her? She wasn't a wanton except for the fact she'd lived with a man ten years unmarried. In her line of work, it wasn't unusual, but the reason Cheyenne society turned their eye was because of Walker and her talent as a singer and actress.

Icefall slowed as they entered the town. She spotted the livery to the right, then the Five Star Saloon. Across the street on the left was the train depot. Callum escorted her to a road on the right where Culpepper's Boarding House resided on the left side of the street. This was it. The town didn't appear menacing as the Scotsman had described, but it was early in the day. Callum secured the horses and extended his hand to assist her out of the buggy. "Thank you for escorting me, but I could have found it on my own."

"Ah, lass, it be no problem." He put her trunk on his shoulder. "Lead the way."

He held her belongings while she paid her money and received a key.

"Upstairs, room eight." Miss Culpepper said as she eyed the Scotsman.

He followed Rose up the stairs and placed the trunk in her room. The space was smaller than his bedroom but held a good-size bed, dresser, table, desk, chair, and washstand. A kerosene lamp and candles stood ready with a box of matches. "Do you want me to take Daisy back to the ranch?"

She opened her trunk and found her red satin dress. "I spotted the livery when we arrived. Will they board my horse and keep my buggy until I need them?"

"Aye, Chet Daniels is trustworthy. I'll take care of it and come back to see you before I go to the ranch." Callum touched the red dress. "Ye be wearing this tonight?"

She held the dress to her body. "I think so, my first night I want to make an impression."

"Depends on your definition of impression." He touched her cheek and left.

****

Callum scurried down the stairs in a stew. The dress reminded him of one the pretty, caramel-skinned Emerald wore on Saturday night at Miss Adelaide's Social Club. Every man in the saloon would have a full view of Rose's breasts and the beautiful pale skin of her neck. "Son of a bitch." He uttered as he lifted the reins and spurred Daisy down Buckboard Alley. He stopped at the left turn on Old Cheyenne Road and stared at Miss Adelaide's place. This was the reason he visited Amethyst on Saturday nights. She tempered his needs, but this woman had all his wants, and he didn't like these new feelings of hunger for another nor the pain it involved.

Chet met him at the entrance to the barn. "You gone all fancy on us, Red?"

He swung down and handed the reins to the owner. "This belongs to a friend of mine—her name's Songbird. Wants you to board the horse and park the buggy here. Says she might need them. I'm paying for a

42

month in advance." He rubbed the horse's head. "The mare's name is Daisy."

"Got it." Chet pocketed the money and guided the horse to a stall. "Would this be the new saloon singer?"

Callum inhaled a deep breath and fisted his hands at his side. "She be the same."

With his business at the livery done, he passed Dugan's Blacksmith Shop. The man nodded, wielding the large hammer against an anvil and a hot metal rod. The loud ding, ding, ding sounded through his ears as he read the notice tacked to a post announcing Songbird would perform at The Five Star Saloon.

A hasty stroll back to the boarding house had him ready to load the redhead and take her back to his house. He returned a menacing stare from Eulalie Culpepper and bolted up the stairs. Rose answered his knock, and he grabbed her and pulled her into a passionate embrace. His mouth found hers. His tongue searched the depths for some kind of answer or assurance. He found none. If he continued, he'd bed her and the pain of leaving her was too great. He backed away and stared at the beauty of the woman before him. "Going to the ranch, but I'll come back tonight. Wouldn't miss your singing debut at the saloon."

"It will be nice to see a friendly face. I don't know why I'm nervous. I've sung in front of thousands, and this is just a little saloon." She held his hand in both of hers. "I don't think I thanked you for all you did for me and Daisy, so I'm saying it now. Thank you, Callum. I wouldn't be alive if not for you."

He rested his chin on the top of her head and nodded his appreciation. He left the room without a word.

Chapter Five

Callum guided Icefall toward the ranch and rode the longest ride of his life. In the past few days, he'd grown accustomed to Rose resting in his home as he worked. Now she lived unprotected in town. He'd never had a woman touch his soul and kindle hope for a future as she had.

The frustration of not having her in his bed every night for the rest of his life, the guilt of leaving her unprotected in Wylder, rage at the man who'd abused her, and—damn!—the love he gave and wanted in return had his life in utter chaos. He drifted down the lane and headed straight to the barn.

Manual labor would soothe his misery. He settled Icefall in his stall and grabbed a pitchfork. The hard work of mucking out the horse stalls caused sweat to bead on his face, and he rolled up the sleeves of his shirt even though the air was still cool. After a quick lunch and water break, the afternoon was spent training the wildest stallion on the ranch.

Daniel watched from outside the arena, his arms rested on top of the fence. "I don't know who's the stubbornest, you or the horse."

The animal reared and let out a loud neigh. He tightened his hold, and the horse relented, but not before he almost dragged the Scotsman to the ground. "This one's got spirit." He paraded him around the arena and wandered toward Daniel.

"Like the red-haired woman you kept at your place." Daniel smiled and let out a chuckle.

He wanted to argue but admitted the truth. "Aye, like that."

Daniel raised his foot to the bottom rail. "Sarah and I were talking. We agree you've met your match with this one."

"So now you're delving into my business." He held the reins tighter.

His friend held up his hand. "Oh, hell, Red, don't go getting mad. We like her. She's the best thing to ever happen in your life. We hope both of you will come to your senses soon and figure it out."

Callum removed the bridle, opened the gate, and urged the horse to the pasture to graze. "She starts work tonight. Going to town to see her perform. Want to go?"

"I need to stay close to home. Don't want to leave Sarah alone." He advanced toward his house. "You have fun and don't start any trouble. Remember, it's her job."

"Why does everyone think I'll cause trouble?" He rolled the leather leads to the bridle in his hands.

Daniel kept walking, shook his head, and waved.

****

The sound of laughter and men heckling each other met him as he dismounted and tied his quarter horse's reins to a post. *Shite*, a full house of drunk rowdy men anxious for a glimpse of Songbird. He entered the Five Star and spotted Russ Holt and approached his friend.

Russ nodded. "Callum. Didn't expect to see you during the week. You here for the new singer? Rumor is she's a beauty."

He didn't answer, just leaned his rifle against the wall and gazed around the place. Men talked and laughed, anxious to see the new woman in town.

Sonny poured the Scotsman a drink of good whiskey. "Don't want no trouble, Callum."

He downed the drink and held the glass for another. "That be up to the others, ye *ken*."

Sonny sat in a chair and put his face even with Callum's. "Hell, no, that be up to you." He stood and swiped grime off the table with a cloth. "Keep an eye on him, Russ."

Russ nodded to the bartender. "What the hell's going on?" He directed the question to the Scottish giant.

"I know the lass. Don't care for her working in a saloon." The firewater burned his throat as he swallowed.

"Son of a bitch, you love this woman." He leaned his head and whispered, "Where'd you meet her? She only arrived in town today."

He scowled and dismissed the comment. "None of your business."

"Sounds like you know her intimately."

Callum scooted his chair back ready to defend Rose's honor. "What I know about her and how I met her is no one's business."

Russ raised both hands. "I'm on your side. Don't want to have to fight the men in here with you, though. Settle your ass down."

Boone Layton sashayed to the piano and played "Carry Me Back to Old Virginny."

A railroader yelled over the music. "We want to see the Songbird."

Boone finished the song and bowed. "Before I introduce our new singer, I want to tell you a little about her. Songbird was born in Ireland but arrived in Wyoming via New York City where she studied voice and honed her skills. We are fortunate she is gracing Wylder with her presence. She's a fine lady, and The Five Star Saloon expects everyone to treat her with the respect she deserves. Welcome, Songbird."

Callum's woman sashayed from the back and made her way to the piano. He almost didn't recognize her. She'd applied make-up with the skill an actor would possess, and her red hair was held atop her head with gold hairpins. The red dress emphasized her creamy breasts, but on her, it seemed in good taste and dignified. The set started with "I Dream of Jeannie with the Light Brown Hair." Her voice was not what he expected. She had a low voice but could sing the high notes with little effort. A rollicking "Camptown Races" brought an end to the show and had everyone singing along. Every man in the saloon leaped from their seats, clapped, whistled, and called her name. Rose bowed, touched her heart, and blew kisses to the men as she made her way to the back room.

"That went well," Russ spoke as he clapped in appreciation of her performance.

"Aye, but the crowd isn't drunk, yet." The men raised their voices in excitement and card games started in earnest.

Boone joined them at the table. "Songbird's the best singer ever to grace The Five Star Saloon and Wylder."

"How many times does she sing?" Callum waved Sonny over for more whiskey.

"Twice a night and early enough so she'll be done before the men get dirty drunk." He walked toward the front. "Gotta tinkle the keys."

Callum relaxed as best he could and played a few hands of poker with Russ. Loud whistles and claps filled the saloon as Songbird entered and curtsied. She sang popular songs and ended with the Irish folk song, "Poor Paddy Works on the Railway." The men whistled and showed their appreciation with loud claps and yells. Rose smiled and scanned the room with her eyes, pausing a moment when her gaze met his. He gave her a slight grin not wanting anyone to know how much he cared. She curtsied, waved, and escaped to the back room.

The Scotsman waited until the clientele settled to the usual drinking and card playing while he kept an eye on her door. He spoke to Russ. "Going to see her to Culpepper's." He grabbed his rifle. "Enjoyed the company."

Russ nodded. "Me, too."

He strolled to the back of the saloon and waited. Rose exited the room with a black lace shawl around her shoulders. "Good evening, lass."

"Callum." She smiled and closed the door.

The crowd spotted Songbird with the Scotsman and shouted Callum's name. A miner yelled, "Now, none of us have a chance."

He put his rifle on his shoulder and escorted Rose through the swinging door of the saloon. As they meandered up the road, he said. "Didn't know ye had such a lovely voice."

She tugged her cape tighter. "You enjoyed the show?"

"I did." When they were out of sight of the saloon, he put his arm around her waist. His logic sparred with his anger. She had to make a living, but to see her on display in a room full of men made his Scottish blood rise to the boiling point. He wanted to see her to her room and make love until tomorrow morning, but he wouldn't lay a hand on her tonight. "Never love a woman in anger," his da told him. The meaning of those words was clear now.

She unlocked the door to room number eight. "Thanks for escorting me."

He gave her a forceful but gentle kiss under the flickering light of a kerosene wall sconce. "Ye be singing tomorrow night?"

"I am." She replied in a whisper.

Callum nodded and waited in the hall until the key turned in the lock.

****

Rose dressed in a plain cotton dress and a straw hat with a wide brim to disguise her appearance. She'd learned the hard way to not draw attention to herself in the light of day, and she'd continue the masquerade she started in Cheyenne.

Sarah Taylor greeted her when she entered Lowery's Dress Shoppe. "Rose, good to see you."

The ladies hugged, but the baby bump kept them from much of an embrace. "Hi, Sarah, didn't expect to see you in town."

"First I've been here in months." Sarah peered around the store and whispered, "How shall I introduce you?"

Rose bit her bottom lip and decided none of Sarah's friends would know anything about her life in

Cheyenne. "You can introduce me using my real name. But I'll still go by Songbird to all the men at the saloon."

Sarah motioned for Mildred Lowery to join them. "Rose, this is my aunt, Mildred Lowery."

The shop owner extended her hand. "I'm Widow Lowery to the town folk."

"Nice to meet you, Widow Lowery. I'm Rose O'Brien."

Mildred stepped behind the counter. "Welcome to Wylder. I 'spect you don't want anyone knowing your real name if'n ya go by Songbird at the saloon." She folded a large piece of lace and placed it on the shelf. "I'll keep your secret."

"Thank you." She paused, aghast that nothing would remain private in this part of Wyoming. "How'd you get to town?"

Sarah found a chair and sat. "Daniel. He's at Wylder Feed and Seed getting supplies."

She had to ask. "Did Callum accompany you?"

Widow Lowery cleared her throat and chuckled.

She hoped Sarah didn't tell the entire town how she'd stayed with Callum, slept in his bed, and let him have his way with her. Sarah couldn't know about the Scotsman bedding her unless he'd spilled the information to Daniel.

The dressmaker gave Sarah a glass of water. "Thank you." She sipped the liquid. "No, he's busy at the ranch. Daniel says he's been working with an ornery stallion for the last few days." She stood and stretched her back. "I told Daniel I don't know who the most ill-tempered one is, Callum or the horse. Since you arrived in Wylder, his temper has reared, and he's not said more than a few words to either of us."

Rose put her hand on her chest. "What's wrong with him?"

Sarah gazed to the ceiling and back to her friend. "He's in love with you, you silly goose."

And she loved him, but it mustn't be. "I'm sure you're mistaken."

She placed the glass on the counter. "Even Aunt Millie agrees, don't you?"

Widow Lowery pursed her lips and nodded her head. "'Bout time someone tamed that handsome Scot."

The people of Wylder sure liked to get into another's business. She chose black, green, and white thread from the spools along the wall and sauntered toward the owner. "I'll take these." She counted out the correct change. "Where can I get decent food?"

Sarah answered, "Right across the street, Jake's Place, serves the best. I was employed there before I married Daniel. I work from home now, doing embroidery for the fine ladies of Wylder."

"Hell's, bells!" the widow squawked. "You mean the fine whores of Wylder. Not many women in this town can afford extra stitching on their dresses except Miss Willowby's crowd."

"You're talking about our good customers. They pay you a good wage for your dresses, and I'm happy to add the special touches." She directed her next comment to Rose. "Amethyst is going to be mad as a wet hen when she finds out about you."

"Who is Amethyst?" The beautiful necklace with the purple stone Walker gave her for her last birthday flashed in her mind, but she'd never met anyone by that name.

Sarah lowered her voice and stepped closer. "Rumor is Callum has been cavorting with Amethyst at the Wylder County Social Club. He's visited her every Saturday night for the last six years."

"I see." If he were in front of her now, she'd bash his head in. She calmed her ire with a laugh. "We aren't a couple. He can see whom he pleases."

"Better tell your face, I've never seen such a scowl as the one you're wearing right now." Sarah touched her arm. "If love finds you, take it by the horns and go with it. I know this for sure—if Callum loved Amethyst, he would have already married her, prostitute or not."

Rose recognized the truth. The Scotsman didn't care about gossip. She pondered this information as a pretty girl advanced from the back of the store.

"Leona, come meet Rose," Sarah said as she motioned the young lady to join them. "Rose O'Brien, this is Leona Fabray. She's a close friend of mine."

Widow Lowery butted in. "She's the washwoman here. We'll be happy to take in your dirties. Leona does a good thorough job."

She greeted the worker. "A pleasure to meet you, Leona." The girl's hair escaped the pins, and her dress twisted around the waist as if she had tugged on the material. Well-worn boots peeked from under her skirt. Leona embodied an innocent quality as if it were hard for her to transition from a girl to a woman. Rose had never done physical labor and acknowledged the work of a washwoman had to be difficult.

"It's a mighty fine pleasure to meet ya." Leona gave her a timid smile. "And I'd be happy to wash your clothes, but now I'm goin' to the hotel to pick up some laundry."

Rose bestowed a grateful smile on the pretty girl. "Thank you, I will need your services."

A red-haired woman with a careworn look entered from the back with a large cloth bag. "Leona, this is ready for the Vincent. Will you take it for me?" She passed the bag to the washwoman.

Sarah called to the worker. "Mary, you must meet Rose, she's from Ireland, too."

Songbird presented her hand. "Rose O'Brien. Nice to meet you, Mary."

The woman extended hers in greeting. "Mary McCleary. I was a Doyle before I married my deceased husband."

The haunting expression in the woman's eyes mirrored her own, and she was glad that Mary's husband was no longer around to abuse her. "O'Brien is my family name. I've never married. It's a pleasure to meet another Irish lady."

Mildred Lowery hastened from the cutting table, and Mary disappeared toward the back of the store. "Mary does the ironing around here and helps Leona with some of the washing."

Of all the people Rose had met in Wylder, Mildred Lowery and Eulalie Culpepper were her least favorite. She wondered if Mrs. Lowery ever smiled, and she got the impression Mary and Leona were worked to the bone. Sarah exuded warmth and generosity, her aunt cold and bitter and for sure a gossip. She offered up a prayer of thanks for having the fortitude to leave Walker before she became a bitter, cold woman. "Thank you for the thread, Widow Lowery, and good to see you, Sarah." Rose exited the store and waited for two wagons to pass before crossing the street to the cafe.

Chapter Six

The food at Jake's Place was hearty and delicious. She dipped the flaky biscuit in the brown beef gravy and finished off the vegetables. The apple pie reminded her of Bessie's delectable desserts, and pain stabbed her gut. Her fondest memories were when Walker traveled and she ate her meals with Homer and Bessie Adams in the kitchen instead of the stodgy dining room.

Bowing her head, she prayed a silent prayer Walker wouldn't fire the couple, or worse, hurt them with his interrogation as to her whereabouts. A few men she recognized from the saloon ate their lunch, but none had a clue of her true identity. By day, she could pass as a farmer's wife in town to buy supplies if her hair stayed pinned and covered with a hat.

Rose paid the waitress and moseyed up Sidewinder Lane. She entered the Outdoor Theater and sat on a bench. She could put on a concert and make extra money for the trip further west. More enticing than making money would be to direct a play with the cast chosen from the people of Wylder. Callum's commanding presence and his voice would make him the perfect choice for the lead male part. She roused herself from her daydreams, left the theater, and strolled by the Vincent House Hotel and Goldmount Bank. Both buildings were built better than any in Wylder and would fit in the city of Cheyenne. The livery was to the right of the town, so she walked down a side road and happened upon the Catholic church. The door stood open and beckoned her to enter. The Sanctuary of Saint Paul's in Cheyenne had been her refuge since her parents died. She entered and searched for a priest to confess her sins but found only a dark quiet space. She blessed herself with the holy water that rested in a white bowl. Candles burned on a side table, and she lit another. The only sound was her feet shuffling on the wood floor.

Rose found her rosary in her reticule and sat on a bench staring at the wooden crucifix hung behind the altar. She made the sign of the cross, prayed the Apostles' Creed, the Our Father, and three Hail Marys. At the beginning of the Hail Mary, she meditated on the prayer for safe travels to her new life in California. When she'd fingered all the beads, her prayers were done. She said the Hail Holy Queen, made the sign of the cross, and left the church.

As Rose approached the livery, she spied a man working on a horse's hoof.

He put his rasp down. "Can I help you, miss?"

"Need to speak to Chet Daniels." She said as she stood on her tiptoes and strained her neck to peek in the stalls.

"That would be me." He wiped his hands on his apron.

"I'm Songbird." She sized up the hardworking man who had an honest appearance and decided he could be trusted. "My real name is Rose O'Brien, and I need to settle my account with you and see my horse, Daisy. Mr. MacPhilip delivered the horse and buggy to you." She held the package of thread between her arm and side and opened her reticule for the money.

"Nice to meet you, Miss O'Brien." He tipped his hat and wiped the sweat off his forehead. "Callum's paid the fees for this month."

She didn't expect that. "I'll settle with him, then." She repositioned the drawstring bag on her arm. "I'd like to see Daisy."

"Of course." He led her inside the barn. "She's in stall five. Anytime you want to see her is fine with me."

Daisy ambled to the gate and stuck her head out. Rose petted her and slipped her a sugar cube. She leaned her face against the mare's head and whispered. "How are you doing, girl?" She addressed the liveryman, "I enjoy riding, so I'll take her out when I can."

"Horses need to be ridden." He paused before he left the barn. "I'll be around if you need me."

Rose found a curry comb and entered the stall. "We made it, girl." Daisy moved her head to acknowledge her master, then nodded and continued to munch on hay. Walker Morgan hated her time with the horse. He'd threatened to sell Daisy, jealous of the time she spent riding and caring for the animal. Any love for Walker faded like the sun burning off a morning fog. One day she loved him and the next she recognized him for what he was. The high price of losing her soul to the man wore her down. One day, courage found her, and she grasped it.

She leaned her head on the horse's side; the familiar smell of hay wafted into her nostrils. "I'll be back soon, and we'll ride." With the gate to the stall secured, Rose sauntered into the bright sunshine. The snow was a memory as the days warmed, but the nights still refused to give up the cold air. The crocheted shawl Bessie had given her for Christmas last year warmed her in more ways than heat.

Rose entered Wylder's Mercantile to examine the goods and kill some time. A tall, handsome, black man with his arms crossed around his middle watched over two women perusing the counter. The ladies got her eye also. They wore satin dresses and perfume so strong it permeated through the store. The dark-skinned woman wore a turquoise dress with embroidery stitched on the skirt. A glance revealed bright green eyes accented by the color of the gown. Her ears perked and she almost dropped her package of thread when the green-eyed woman addressed the other.

"Amethyst, what do you mean you don't think this hat is pretty? It would be a perfect match for your new dress." She placed it on the woman's head.

Rose stood two aisles over and pretended to browse for gloves but instead studied the prostitute from her head to her feet. Amethyst was buxom, with long, thick dark hair and eyes as blue as the sky. Her hands shook and breaths burst from her lungs hard and fast. She'd made excuses for living with Walker but in truth, she was no better than these women. She succeeded in her escape of one lover only to find another before arriving at her destination. She crouched behind the tall shelf and focused her eyes toward the interaction.

"I don't like it. Let's go to Lowery's Dress Shoppe." Amethyst placed the hat on the table and addressed the towering man. "We're ready to leave, Abraham."

He opened the door and escorted them out.

Rose closed her eyes and drank air into her lungs. So, this was Callum's lover. Did he return to the Social Club after their tryst? She told herself it didn't matter, there could be no future between them, but her heart refused the message. Did he tell her he loved her in the heat of passion as he'd done when they were abed? Did he call her his love? His Gaelic words tattooed in her brain. Unable to move, her fingers clung to the shelf as her brain replayed the Scotsman's words of love.

An older gentleman approached. "Good afternoon, I'm Finn Wylder. May I be of assistance?"

She severed her hands from the shelf, let them fall to her side, and presented him with a practiced smile. "I'm Rose O'Brien, new to town. Thought I'd check out your store."

"If you don't see what you want, I can order from Denver and have it in a week." He stepped to the front of the Mercantile.

Rose spent the rest of the day in her room fuming and imagining all sorts of scenarios. Callum could visit the social club any time he wanted; he could be there right now. The prostitute suited the Scotsman more than she did. Amethyst was taller and had more curves. Furious from the newfound knowledge, she decided, if he liked wanton women, she could play the part.

****

Callum studied his poker hand and glanced at Russ and the two railroad men. The younger of the trainmen had a tell, and his bouncing leg almost knocked the table over. "I raise." He threw more money in the pot.

The three men conceded and threw their cards down.

The Scotsman checked the time on his pocket

watch. "Last hand, gentlemen." He raked in his earnings.

The two men departed and found another table.

Russ peeked at the winner's cards. "Damn, Callum, you've got a poker face. Your hand wasn't worth a shit dime." Russ stacked the cards to the side of the table.

A whistle sounded through the saloon as Songbird entered the room. A thin silver boa wrapped around her neck and drifted to her cleavage. Tonight, her hair flowed down her back in waves, her lips as red as her tresses. Silver earrings sparkled from her ears to her shoulders. This costume wasn't elegant it was whorish. Son of a bitch, he wanted to get her out of here now.

The whistles and shouts continued until Boone stood in a chair and yelled over the crowd. "Show the lady some respect or she won't sing for you."

The banter died down, and every eye focused on Songbird.

Callum stewed through the entire performance. He wanted to take off his shirt and throw it over her. When she bowed, the boa and the cleavage along with her hair tumbled toward her face.

As she straightened from her bow, their eyes met, hers shot daggers in his direction. What the hell was she mad about?

Rose's performance was over, and he wasted no time getting to the door she entered and waited, rifle in hand. Several men had followed him desperate to see her, but he sent them back to their seats. He slipped money to Sonny and told him to give drinks to the threatening men to keep them from following her.

Callum lumbered close beside her. Men scooted their chairs away from tables ready to approach, but his deadly stare and the rifle slung over his shoulder kept them in their seats. When they were in the street he asked. "You want to tell me why you're mad at me?"

"I'm not angry with you, you can do whatever the hell you want. You're a grown man." She wandered away from him.

He grabbed her arm to stop her. "What are ye talking about?"

She struggled and wrung herself free of his grasp. "You know what I'm referring to." She spat the words.

"Ah *dinnae ken.*" He gazed into her green eyes. "I don't like the way you're dressed tonight. You look like a whore."

A slap hit his face. The contact didn't hurt him, but the action pierced his soul like an arrow. "Lass, what is wrong with you?"

"I'm sorry, Callum." She wiped tears from both sides of her face.

He wrapped one arm around her shoulder still holding the rifle in the other. "*Mo ghràdh.* I don't know who has hurt you, but I promise you, I will not." He escorted her through the starlit night to the boarding house.

They entered her room, and he led her to the bed, lit the candle on the table, and sat in a chair. "Tell me, lass."

She tugged each finger of her gloves and set the boa and elbow-length gloves on the table. "The town vibrates with gossip about the prostitute you visit every week. One you've been seeing since you arrived in Wyoming. I saw her at the Mercantile with her friend and their escort. If you want a whore, then go to Amethyst. Leave me be."

"Yer talkin' mince withoot a *tattie* in sight." He spoke in his native tongue.

"It is not nonsense." She glared.

He laughed. "So, you do understand Gaelic. I'll have to watch what I say around you."

She stood and crossed her arms over her chest. "You think this is a joke?"

He stood and peered down at the beautiful red-haired woman. "No, lass." He pointed at her and then at himself. "We are not a joke. The emotion, the feeling, the yearning I have for you are real and it's serious."

He gathered her in his arms and kissed her. She pounded his chest with her fists and fought him, but when his tongue entered her mouth, she gave up the resistance as he claimed her lips over and over. He whispered in her ear. "Ye be mine, Rose, ye be mine." He held her until her breathing calmed and her tension released. Callum kissed her forehead. "How could I even think of another woman after you?"

She left his embrace. "I'm sorry for the way I acted. I don't know why I became so jealous. We've just met, and I have my career to think about."

"Career?" Callum rubbed the back of his head and swallowed anger. Anger at her, at Walker Morgan, at himself for not being able to protect her in Wylder. "Respectfully, Rose, I don't think ye'll have much of a career in Wylder, Wyoming."

"I know." She waved her hand. "I don't plan to stay here."

Her words yielded a blow to his gut. "Where will you go?"

She dropped her head in her hands. "I don't know."

He held her close with her head resting on his

chest. Her long hair caressed his calloused hands like fine silk. "Ye've had a rough time. Don't make a decision ye'll regret."

He closed his eyes and breathed in her rose perfume. Her scent and quiet spirit calmed the raging fire he didn't know existed until her. "I don't want to leave you with animosity in our hearts. I want the best for you."

Rose whispered, "Thank you. I owe you my life."

"Shhh." He tugged her hair behind her ear and lowered his head. "Everything will be fine." After a quick kiss on her lips, he slipped out the door.

Chapter Seven

Weeks passed since Rose arrived in Wylder and not a day went by that she didn't remember her life in Cheyenne. She worried about Homer and Bessie Adams, who had become as close as family to her. The sweet lady had encouraged her to leave Walker after she treated the first laceration to Rose's face. They never admitted what a bad person Mr. Morgan was, but unsaid words spoke louder than real ones in this case. Miles Barron, the young stagehand, had Daisy and the carriage ready in the early morning hours and helped her get her trunk to the buggy. He asked to accompany her, but she didn't want him to be any more involved than he was. She'd not said goodbye to the old couple, and it broke her heart. She didn't miss the mansion and fine furnishings, her little room in the boarding house was safe, and though somewhat lonely, it enveloped her like a warm cloak in the winter.

Rose entered Lowery's Dress Shoppe to collect Leona for tea at Laurel Holt's house. Sarah would be in attendance, and she couldn't wait to see her new friend. She entered the store and Leona ran, then stopped, held her head high, and strolled toward her. "Good afternoon, Rose."

She smiled at the beautiful young lady. Leona reminded her of a wild mare almost tamed but the wild not wanting to go quiet. "Leona, you are lovely today.

Your hair pinned on your head emphasizes your pretty face."

"Gambler tol' me the same thing." She lifted a basket from the table. "I'm ready to go."

Widow Lowery wandered from the back with another basket. "Bought these vanilla cakes from the bakery. Sarah loves them. I'm sure she's craving all sorts of food now."

Rose positioned her arm through the basket handle. "I wish you could join us."

Mildred straightened stacks of fabric on the shelf. "You young ladies need some gossip time to yourselves without an old woman listening in. But if there's anything new, I expect Leona will tell me tomorrow."

They walked to the livery, Chet had Daisy and the carriage ready.

"Thank you, Mr. Daniels," Rose said as she climbed in the buggy.

He tipped his hat. "Safe travels." He passed the reins and stepped aside.

The women settled into the leather seat and Rose guided Daisy to Old Cheyenne Road. The weather was beautiful, the sky blue with a few white clouds, and the bright sun saturated the day with warmth. Her carriage had a top and shielded them from the sun's rays and the heat.

Leona searched for the lane. "It's up a little way. Next to the big cedar tree on the right."

Rose hadn't been back to the ranch since the snow, and she marveled at the beautiful landscape. The buggy traveled under the arch, and she read the sign,

Lex Taylor Ranch
Daniel Taylor and Callum MacPhilip, Proprietors

Sarah stood on the front porch with a napkin-covered plate. Daniel waited beside her. She tugged Daisy to a stop in front of the house.

Daniel helped Sarah down the stairs and assisted her into the buggy. "Rose, Leona." He nodded his head.

"Afternoon, Daniel," Rose said and scanned the ranch for her Scotsman.

"Callum's in the back pasture with the horses." Daniel grinned at Rose.

Her face heated in embarrassment that her thoughts were so obvious. "Of course."

Daniel mounted his horse and followed them to the Holt Ranch. When they arrived, he helped his bride out of the carriage. "You ladies have fun, and I'll be back in a few hours." He kissed his wife on the cheek and rode off toward his ranch.

Laurel greeted them. A little boy clung to the folds of her dress with a chicken beside him. Sarah and Leona hugged her. She grabbed Rose and drew her close. "Rose, I've heard so much about you. It's a pleasure to have you for tea. I've been looking forward to spending the afternoon with you all."

Leona squatted and placed her hands on the child's shoulders. "Hi, Jesse." The boy hugged her, and she kissed his cheek.

Sarah patted his head. "Jesse, I'd love to kiss you, but I can't bend over." The child laughed and ran to the front room, followed by the chicken.

"Put the food on the table in front of the settee," Laurel instructed as they entered.

The hostess's belly appeared a little smaller than Sarah's. Rose almost asked if she was with child, but an infant's cry stilled her words.

Laurel addressed Leona. "Will you help me with the babies?"

"I sure will. Been missing them little fellers." She followed Laurel up the stairs.

When they were alone, she addressed Sarah. "Babies?"

Sarah arranged the scones, cookies, and cakes on the China plates. "She had twins, should be about six weeks old now."

The women entered the room; each held a baby. They stopped in front of Rose, and Laurel beamed. "These are my twin boys, Richard and Russell."

She stared at the handsome babies with fists raised and legs kicking free of their gowns. One of them let out a wail and the other followed. "They're precious. I can't imagine having two at the same time."

Sarah plopped down on the sofa. "Me either." She addressed Laurel. "How do you feel?"

"Never better. Doc Sullivan says my body will be back to normal soon. I aim to get at least a little bit of my girlish figure back." She sat in a large chair and unbuttoned her dress. "I hope you don't mind, they're hungry and I don't want to waste a minute of our time together." Leona passed the crying boy, and Laurel adjusted each baby to a nipple.

Rose had never seen a woman feed a child from her breast. A dull pain started in her chest and a tear slid down her face. She brushed it away before the ladies noticed. Sarah large with child and Laurel holding her babes to her breast made Rose doubt she'd make it through the afternoon. She'd wanted a child for the last five years of her thirty. Prayed to the Virgin Mary and all the Saints in Heaven that Walker would marry her, and they would have a child. She'd found the courage to mention it, and he responded, "Well if you get in the family way, I'll consider marrying you." This was the start of their demise and her incentive to escape.

"Do you know how to burp a baby, Leona?" Laurel asked as she adjusted the children on her lap and buttoned her dress.

"Tell me what to do, and I will. I need the practice in case me and Gambler get married." She gathered Richard in her arms and settled him in her lap.

Laurel gave her a towel. "Put the cloth on your shoulder and hold the baby like this and pat its back. You'll hear it. Sometimes they spit up a bit." She placed a cloth over her shoulder and demonstrated with little Russell.

Leona did the same and laughed out loud when the baby expelled a loud burb. "I did it."

Rose surveyed the space. Two cradles sat on either side of the door, a sewing machine, desk, settee, chairs, and toys filled the space. Jesse sat on the floor playing. She'd almost forgotten about him. Under the window, the chicken sat in a wooden box filled with hay. She sat straighter in her seat and stared at the bird.

Laurel rocked the baby in her arms and laughed. "Rose, meet Harold, Jesse's pet chicken."

"I've never known anyone with a pet chicken." This was the home of a family; something she'd never have.

Laurel and Leona settled the babies in their cradles and collected teapots from the kitchen. "Let's have our tea and talk."

Rose poured tea into porcelain cups and passed

them around. "Who is Gambler?" She took a sip of hot tea and stared at Leona over the rim of her teacup. "I've known you for weeks now and you've never mentioned him until today.

Sarah interrupted. "Dalton Payne."

"Dalton Payne." Rose's teacup stopped on the way to her lips. "He's your beau?"

Leona crossed her arms and sat on the edge of the settee. "He shore is, and how do you know him?"

Her new friend showed a jealous side, and she didn't blame her. Dalton Payne was a handsome man, famous for his prowess in the gambling world. He'd won more championships than anyone in the history of poker. She and Walker were invited to watch him play in Cheyenne. "I didn't know he lived in Wylder."

"He's got a farm outside town where he lives with his son Gideon." She put a scone on her plate.

"Didn't know he had a boy." Rose eyed Leona, not wanting to cause more ire from her.

"He adopted him." She settled in her seat and bit into a cookie. "We're gonna be a family soon as Dalton gets over his knee surgery. Says he won't marry me till he's healed."

"Guess he wants everything to be in good working order for the honeymoon." Sarah put a hand over her mouth to silence her chuckle.

"Gambler may have a bum knee but ain't nothin' else broke." She added, "'Ceptin' those two beds he had to fix."

"Leona." Laurel scolded, then added, "Tell us more."

"We ain't doin' nothin' y'all don't do." She crossed her arms over her chest and dipped her head toward Laurel and Sarah. "You two are the proof. Do it enough, and a baby won't be far behind."

The words cut Rose's gut like a knife. She forced a smile and swallowed more tea.

Sarah leaned into her chair and rubbed her belly. "Callum is mighty smitten with you. He's been to town near every day and doesn't come back 'til late at night, and a few times he returned in the early morning."

Heat prickled through her face as she recalled their late nights and early mornings of lovemaking. The handsome Scotsman doing things no other had ever done. She'd done things she would never have done with Walker. "He's escorted me to my room every night since I started my job at the saloon." She glanced at the women. "Says he worries about me being alone."

Sarah scrutinized the table of food. "Wylder is a dangerous place, for sure, but he needs every man to know he's staked his claim." She placed a vanilla cake on her plate. "I miss these sweets."

"Widow Lowery sent them to you," Leona chimed in.

"Please, tell her thank you. I've been craving them." Sarah placed another on her plate.

Laughter and talk of husbands, a soon-to-be husband, babies, gossip, and the handsome Scotsman filled the afternoon. Rose enjoyed her visit with the women. The babies were awake, and she held Russell, amazed at his soft skin and bright eyes. Jesse stood beside her; his small hand rubbed the child's head. "You love your baby brother?" She addressed the little boy.

He nodded and ran to Leona, who held Richard.

Laurel rested against the back of her chair while

the women held her babies. "We named Russell after Caleb's uncle…I mean father. Russ is so excited about the twins being the namesake for him and his brother. Caleb still calls him Uncle Russ; out of habit, I suppose."

Rose gazed into the eyes of the squirming infant. "Russ is Callum's friend. They play poker together every night. Such a nice man."

"Yes, he lives here on the ranch. He treats me like a daughter, and adores Jesse, too." A grin spread on her face as her husband entered the room.

Caleb approached Laurel's chair and kissed her on the cheek. "You ladies having a good afternoon?" He scooped Jesse in his arms.

"We've had a wonderful time." Sarah stood and stretched. "I think I sat too long." She wandered around the room and glanced out the window. "Daniel's here."

Caleb excused himself. "I'll visit with Daniel till y'all are ready to leave."

Leona and Rose worked to clear the table of plates and the pretty tea service. "We'll put everything in the kitchen," Leona lifted the heavy tray. "Won't take long to get these washed."

Rose dried and stacked the service wear. "I'm so happy for you and Dalton, Leona."

The washwoman rinsed a plate. "I love him, and he loves me. Never expected it. He's making me a lady. Still not used to wearing a dress most days, but it's growin' on me." She dried her hands with a cloth. "I'd do anything to please him."

Rose hugged her. "Leona, you are so beautiful and sweet, Dalton wants you to shine."

"You and the Scotsman are good together. I've

seen the two of you in town. Y'all match like Sarah and Daniel, and Laurel and Caleb. My ma always said there's someone for everyone. Just have to look for 'em." She dried her hands. "Glad I found mine."

Rose couldn't remember a happier day than this, surrounded by friends and sharing her new life in Wylder with them. "I'm glad you found yours, too."

Chapter Eight

The wind swept through Rose's hair and tugged at the ribbons securing her hat as she rode her horse alongside Finlay toward the ranch. The sky sported a few clouds announcing a possibility of rain, and the air held to the chilly early spring wind. Callum kept his quarter horse at a canter, so she followed suit even though she wanted to lead Daisy to a gallop and let the wind take her and the trials of the last month.

"Ye ride like ye were born to it." He slowed his horse and the mare followed.

"We didn't come to the States until I was nine. I learned to ride on a pony named Innis. By the time we left, I had a horse. I had to leave Tully behind. I still miss him." She gave him a sideways glance and pulled on the reins to guide her horse around a fallen limb. "And you, do you miss your homeland?"

"No, I believe home is wherever I am at the time. This is my place, now." He nodded toward her horse. "Ye have a good mare, well taken care of."

She patted the horse on the neck. "I've had her since I arrived in Cheyenne, eleven years ago."

Callum led them to his house. They dismounted and tied the reins to the hitching post. "Gonna show you around the ranch, but I need to get something first."

Rose rested her hand on the porch rail. "The miners and railroad men drink, play poker, and spend their money at the saloon on Friday night. My entertainment interfered with Sonny's revenue, so I now have Fridays off."

"Is that so?" He placed his arm around her waist. "Ye be staying the night with me, then." He turned her face up and kissed her.

"I'd like that." She tiptoed and surrendered to his possessive kiss.

Callum entered the house and grabbed a saddlebag. "We'll ride to the stable first, want to show you my Clydesdale mare."

They entered the large barn. He stopped at a stall and introduced Duchess. "This is my first mare. She'll foal soon and be the start of the draft horse business." He opened the gate and they entered.

She rubbed the animal's head and spoke. "Such a beautiful lady. My father had a Clydesdale in Ireland."

Callum led the mare outside. "Gonna put her to pasture for the day."

"This is a beautiful ranch. What's the significance of the name Lex Taylor? Why not MacPhilip Taylor?" She trudged beside him toward the fenced-off area.

"Daniel's from Lexington, Kentucky. His father breeds racehorses. I worked for them until we traveled west. Daniel borrowed the money from his parents to start the ranch, thus the name Lex Taylor." He opened the pasture gate.

Rose stared at the beauty of the land with horses grazing in the flat green meadow. Mares and foals dotted the landscape. "Where are the stallions?"

"We have them in another pasture." He put his arm on her back and led her to the barn. "We'll stop there on our way to the creek."

She mounted Daisy, and they rode down a trail. The snowcapped mountains in the distance reminded her of the day of her rescue. Now, she lived in constant fear Walker would find her. She'd rehearsed what she'd say if he found her and assured herself he couldn't make her go back. They weren't married, and she now understood why God and the saints had not answered her prayers.

Callum dismounted first and held Daisy's reins while she eased to the ground. "Here's our male stock."

Icefall sauntered to the fence, and she rubbed his neck and placed her head against his. "I miss the draft horses. Happy to see you breed them."

"Good horses for heavy work. We've advertised in Denver and Cheyenne, already getting inquiries. I think we'll have more requests than we have stock. I have another stallion and mare arriving by train soon."

They mounted their horses. Rose spurred Daisy to a gallop and Finlay raced beside them. She leaned into the wind, one with the mare. The wind whipped past her ears, and the sound of the horse's hooves pounding the ground produced a smile to her face and freedom to her soul. On her rides she and Daisy only ventured a short way from Wylder down Old Cheyenne Road. She'd remembered the warnings from Leona and Sarah. Both had been accosted by bad men.

Finlay slowed, and she tugged the reins to steady her horse. A stream flowed through the landscape, the water rippled over rocks, and early spring wildflowers bloomed white and purple along the edge. They descended from their saddles, and he let the horses go free so they could get a drink from the fresh water.

He gathered her in his arms and swung her around

like a rag doll. The exhilaration and freedom had her giggling and kicking her feet. "Put me down." She laughed, not meaning the words. He claimed her lips, the passion so intense she wasn't sure if the movement caused her dizziness or the kiss. The man's hold on her heart was strong. She could never hurt him or say no to anything he asked—anything except the question of marriage. The Scotsman deserved more than her. She slid to the ground in front of him; her body brushed against the bulge in his pants. Her core contracted, wanting, needing, craving the connection.

He pulled them to the ground, his hat tumbled off his head, and she stumbled, her legs tangled in her dress. After the laughter subsided, he tugged her hat off her head. "*Tà mo chroi istigh ionat.*"

The Gaelic words broke her heart. Before she could stop herself, she uttered. "And I you, Callum." The words fueled a fire. Her body burned for his touch while he made love to her on the cold ground, their coupling urgent as he drove into her over and over until she screamed in release. The power of the moment felt as if her body hovered in the cool morning air, suspended above the earth and below the heavens.

"Rose, *mo ghràdh.*" Spent, Callum lay on his back with her atop him.

She rested on his huge body. Even in lovemaking he placed her comfort above his. If things were different, she'd give in to his request of marriage, but she was thirty, and if she were not with child by now, she'd never be. "You're going to get cold." She scolded.

He explored her mouth with his tongue. His desire to have her again evident in his sighs. "Callum

MacPhilip, are you ever satiated?" She jumped to standing.

"Not when it comes to my Wylder Rose, I'm not." He fastened the buttons on his pants. "I've got you all day and all night. There'll be time for more loving."

Rose adjusted her dress and removed stray leaves and grass from her hair. The horses grazed beside the stream, and she followed Callum to his horse where he removed the saddlebag containing their food. He passed her a large cloth. "What's for lunch?" She walked toward a grassy spot beside the stream and settled the white material on the ground.

"Biscuits and ham," he said as he grabbed a canteen from the saddle. "Apples for us and the horses." He stuffed the fruit in his pocket.

They finished their meal and drank water. He extended his hand and helped her stand. They danced as he sang "Loch Lomond." She sang harmony just as she'd done with her Papa on the old Scottish folk tune. She sang a low alto harmony on most of the song, but in the last chorus, she let her soprano sing a high harmony over his manly Scottish baritone. Their voices echoed into the morning air beside the babbling creek, a more perfect moment she'd never spent.

At the end of the song, he drew her closer. "Marry me, me bonnie lass."

She closed her eyes and rested her head on his chest. Her heart screamed yes, but she shook her head. "I can't."

He placed his hands on her shoulders and gazed into her eyes. "I know not why ye say no. I *dinnae* wanna rush you. I *ken* you've been hurt, and I can wait till ye heal."

****

Callum rode alongside Rose as they returned to the barn. Her words, *And I you, Callum*, surged through his blood. She'd declared the words so softly he questioned his hearing, but his heart heard them loud and clear. He let Daisy get ahead so he could watch. She sat in the saddle like a queen, so confident and sure of herself. He wanted to spend the rest of his life with her, grow old with her, protect her, love her, sleep with her in his arms every night until he died of old age. He'd not give up—the bond between them was too strong, and he'd unravel the mystery of her, one thread at a time.

Chapter Nine

The sun inched above the horizon as Callum and Daniel rode their quarter horses toward Cheyenne. Henri Dubois, a draft horse rancher from Canada, would arrive on the afternoon train with four Clydesdales—three mares and a stallion. Callum and Henri had remained in close communication since the ranchers had discovered Duchess hailed from his horse farm in Ottawa. The horses would take a long journey by train from Canada to New York and then New York to Cheyenne. Callum slowed Finlay and eased toward Kentucky. "Boone told me where Walker Morgan lives, going to ride by his house and the theater, see if I can get sight of him."

Daniel drew in the reins and stopped his horse. "You think that's wise, Red?"

"Aye." He held tight to Finlay's reins. "Need to know the man's appearance in case he comes to Wylder searching for Rose."

Daniel let out a deep breath. "Watch your temper, and if you see him, don't say anything. I know you'd like nothing better than a confrontation, but you must think of Rose's safety."

"Agreed. Ye be right." Callum spurred his quarter horse to a slow gallop toward Cheyenne, Kentucky keeping the pace.

He followed the piano player's directions to

Sycamore Road and spotted the large two-story mansion where Walker Morgan lived. The affluent area of Cheyenne sported two- and three-story homes with wide porches and fancy carriages. Though the winter was beginning to change to spring, the lawns were green, and flowers sported the front walks. "Fancy houses." Callum dismounted a block away and pretended to check his horse while sneaking glances at the house.

Daniel swung from his saddle and held the reins. "Money." He pretended to check his saddlebag. "Seems this Walker Morgan is very wealthy."

The street was busy with people milling around in carriages and strolling the sidewalks, so they relaxed and studied the fancy homes. A large carriage waited beside Walker's house with the driver seated in the front. An older gentleman placed a small trunk in the buggy and retreated into the house. The driver, a tall, thin but muscular man in his twenties climbed down from his perch; two six-guns in a low holster rested on his thighs. He opened the door to the covered carriage for the tall older man dressed in a long coat and top hat carrying a cane. "That's the bastard," Callum whispered.

"Let's follow him," Daniel mounted his stallion.

They allowed two wagons to pass and followed behind until Morgan's carriage arrived at the theater. Their horses sauntered past, and Callum got a clear vision of the old man's face and his driver. "I have their faces engrained in me brain." He swung his horse around and Daniel followed. "We're going back to his house."

The Scotsman wanted more information, and he'd

get it from Homer and Bessie Adams. "Rose told me about the couple who took care of her. According to her, they don't care much for Walker Morgan but at their age have no place else to go."

They rode to Pine Street, the street behind Sycamore, and dismounted. Callum passed his reins to Daniel. "Wait here. I'm going to the back, talk to the housekeeper and butler. They were Rose's friends. I know they're worried about her. Also, want to see if Walker has an inkling where she is."

Daniel quieted the horses. "Careful, Red." He nodded to the rifle resting in the scabbard. "Not taking that?"

"No, got a derringer in my pocket, rifle is too obvious." He ambled toward the back of the house, alert for any trouble.

The butler was in the backyard cultivating a small patch of ground with a hoe. He spotted Callum and stopped. "Good day. Might I be of help to you?"

"Mr. Adams, Homer Adams?" Callum stood several feet away.

"Who's asking?" The old man leaned on the garden hoe.

He drew closer and opened his hands in front of him. "I'm Callum MacPhilip, a friend of Rose O'Brien. Don't mean you any harm, just need a little information, and I have some for you."

Homer let the hoe drop to the ground. "Is the dear girl all right?"

"Aye, she be fine. She told me about you and your wife and of your love and care. She's sorry she didn't say goodbye." He surveyed the area on alert for trouble. "I won't tell you where she is, but the lass is safe."

"Safe for now." He wandered closer. "The master's got men searching, and when they find her, directions are to deliver her back. Wants to make her suffer for leaving and making him a laughingstock." He removed his hat and wiped his brow. "He's always been a mean son of a bitch, but since she left, he drinks heavier and brings women here and beats them when he's done getting his pleasure. A despicable man."

Callum clenched his fist. He should kill Morgan today. He deserved to die after what he'd done to Rose, and now other innocent women were paying a high price for the attention of one of the richest men in Cheyenne. He swallowed his temper and examined the large house. "Thank you for the information. Tell your wife Rose be fine."

"One more thing." Mr. Adams lowered his voice. "His driver is his enforcer; anyone crosses Mr. Morgan is hurt…or worse." Homer stared at the sky then into Callum's eyes. "His name is Willard Clayton. He's an ex-gunslinger." He picked up his hoe. "We never had this talk."

Callum nodded and made his way to Pine Street and his horse. He told Daniel of the conversation and made plans for Rose's protection. The stubborn woman wouldn't leave Wylder, wouldn't marry him, wouldn't give up her job at the saloon, wouldn't listen to reason. She needed twenty-four-hour surveillance at all times. "I'm going to the Pinkerton Agency. We've time before the train arrives." He swung his leg over his mount.

"Good idea." The riders navigated the busy streets to the detective bureau.

They tied their reins to the hitching post in front of the building. "Let's see what they can do for us."

Callum entered the building followed by Daniel.

A young woman sat at a desk entering information into a large book. She put her pen down and addressed the men. "May I help you?"

The Scotsman held his Stetson by the brim. "Need to hire a detective."

A man appeared at the desk and passed the girl a stack of papers. "Felix Ross. Come to my office."

They followed him to a room with dark wood paneling, a large desk, and a window view of the back alley. The room was lit with four kerosene lamps; the light competed with the dark walls and the small window.

Mr. Ross closed the door and set two chairs in front of his desk. "How may I help you?"

Callum explained the situation with Rose and inquired about a detective shadowing her. "I don't feel the lass is safe alone in Wylder, but she mustn't find out I've hired ye. In Cheyenne, she was with Walker Morgan and I *ken* he's no good. I have it on good authority he and his men are already searching the territory. It's a matter of time before they find her." Callum leaned in his seat and gazed at the notes. "Better put Willard Clayton's name down. He's Walker's enforcer."

At the mention of the two names, Mr. Ross stopped taking notes and glanced at the two men. He relaxed in his chair and crossed his arms over his chest. "I see. Yes, I know Rose O'Brien, seen her perform at the theater." He leaned forward and took more notes. "I'll be your detective on this case. When do you want me to start?"

Callum didn't miss the recognition in the

detective's eyes when he mentioned Morgan and Clayton. "How do I know Walker Morgan hasn't already hired the Pinkertons to find her?"

Felix lifted his pencil from the paper and held it suspended in the air. "I assure you, that is not the case. You have our complete trust. We will do everything to keep Miss O'Brien safe. Now, I have a few more questions for you." He continued writing notes on his pad.

Callum answered inquiries about Rose's clothes, work, friends, living arrangements, schedule, habits, and family history. "I'm in town as much as I can be, but we have a ranch to run, and Rose is independent, doesn't like people hanging on her."

Felix shook their hands. "I'll see you in Wylder. I take on disguises so I can fit in and often change my appearance."

The men stood to leave, but Mr. Ross continued talking. "The fewer who know about you hiring me, the better. I'll notify the sheriff when I get to town, but I expect you to give him a rundown of the situation beforehand. If there's any trouble, I like to have the sheriff and deputy know I'm on their side."

"Yes, sir." Callum nodded as he left the room.

The trek back to the ranch was slow. Each rancher led two Clydesdales to the Lex Taylor without incident. The large animals had a good temperament like Icefall and Duchess and adjusted to their new stalls, chomping on hay and oats. "We'll turn them out to pasture in the morning. Let them get used to the barn and the sounds of the others first." Callum and Daniel leaned on the gate and admired their new purchases. The Scotsman petted the mare's face. "Gonna get cleaned up and get to town for tonight's performance."

Daniel meandered from the barn. "I'll milk the cow. You get to town before it gets late."

"Appreciate it." The Scotsman raced to his home and got himself ready for the late night. It had been a long day and would be an even longer night staying at the saloon until Songbird finished her shows. His first stop in Wylder was the livery, where he chatted with Chet Daniels and left Icefall tied to a post with plenty of water and hay in a trough. Next, he stopped by the sheriff's office.

Sheriff Branch Wylder was out in the territory, but the deputy noted the information and promised to be on the lookout for any trouble from outsiders. He planned to keep his word to Felix Ross except for Boone and Russ. Boone would be in danger if they found Rose, since he was instrumental in getting her a job in Wylder. Russ roamed through town from visits to Adelaide Willowby, his love at the Social Club, and to the bakery to satisfy his sweet tooth. He was observant and a good ally. No one would suspect him of being a spy.

The Scotsman eyed the crowded saloon for trouble. Satisfied all were familiar faces, he moseyed to the table with his friends—Russ Holt fellow rancher, Coyote Sullivan the town doctor, and Dalton Payne ex-poker champion—and leaned his rifle against the wall. "Count me in." He sat in a chair and placed money on the table. Dalton shuffled the deck in his slick way, sliding the cards along the table with little effort. "Don't know why we bother to play with you." Callum chuckled as he studied his cards.

Dalton sat back from the table with his bad leg

stretched out. "This is a game of poker with friends." He threw a dollar in the money stack.

"Shit." Russ threw his cards on the table. "I'm out."

A brown Stetson rested on Coyote's head, and he lowered his face to gaze into the cards in his hand. "I'll raise you."

Callum threw money in the pot and stared at the dealer. "I'll call. What say ye, Gambler?"

Dalton laid down his cards. "Two pair."

"Three eights." Coyote put both hands in the middle of the table ready to take the money.

Callum placed his cards down one by one. "Full house." With a big smile, he raked the money toward him and stuffed it in his pocket.

A soft hand rested on his shoulder, and he swiveled his head to find Amethyst standing behind him. Songbird would be out for her show in a few minutes, and the last thing he wanted her to see was the prostitute hanging on his arm.

He hurried to guide her outside when Rose exited the backroom. She froze and her gaze flew from Amethyst to him. Poisoned arrows flew from her eyes and pierced his own. She regained her composure, blossomed into the saloon singer, and sashayed to the stage, nodding and smiling at the men's claps and yells.

He tightened his hold on Amethyst and escorted her into the night. "What do you want, lass?"

The prostitute slid her breasts against his chest and stroked his manhood with her hand. "I want you."

His erection grew from her familiar touch. It was a natural reaction, but it caused guilt to rise in his gut. "Amethyst, we were just a Saturday night liaison. You were nothing more to me, and I'm sorry if you had a different idea."

She settled close and rubbed against his hardness. "I feel something different. Tell me you don't want it from me." She purred in his ear. "Come with me, now." Amethyst kissed the place on his neck that drove him wild. "I'll do all the things you like. It's been some time, and I know you miss me." She grabbed his hand and tugged him toward the Wylder County Social Club.

He stood like a tree, unbending and unmoving. "I'm sorry, lass. I *dinnae* mean to hurt you, but I'm with Rose O'Brien, and I plan to marry her."

The prostitute's chin quivered, and tears ran down her face. "But…but I love you. You've been with none but me for years… I hoped…" She fell against his chest.

The Scotsman put his arm on her back. "Shhh." His fingers tangled in her hair and her scent filled his nostrils. How many times had he taken this woman? They had a history, and if not for Songbird, he might have married her, but he didn't love her as he did his Irish lass, and never would. "Let me get you back home." He led her to the brothel.

The night was dark, with stars twinkling overhead and a sliver of moonlight. Callum kept his hand on the woman's arm, guiding her to the familiar club, the one where he'd enjoyed many a night of talk, laughter, singing, and companionship. The Social Club had been more than a place to release his sexual desire, and Amethyst, God bless her soul, had been an important part of his life. He should have told her. She deserved more than being treated like his whore. She sat in the chair, and he leaned against the porch rail. "I should have told you. I'm sorry."

"You can't love her more than me, you can't." He passed her his handkerchief, and she wiped the tears from her face. "She's no different from me. I may be a whore, but she's a saloon singer who would open her legs for any man…" She stopped talking, stood and kissed Callum's cheek. "You'll come back to me, and I'll be waiting."

"No, lass. I won't be back." He opened the door and stepped aside to let her enter. "And you're wrong about Rose O'Brien. She's a lady." He tipped his hat. "Goodbye, Amethyst."

Callum settled in one of the rocking chairs that lined the front porch of the brothel. He was an arse, and he disliked himself for not recognizing her feelings. He sat and stared into the dark of the night as he weighed his options. The prostitute was wrong. He wouldn't be back. If he couldn't have his Songbird, he wanted no one. The image of any other woman but Rose lying beneath him wouldn't even form in his brain. He'd have his Wylder Rose or no one at all.

Chapter Ten

A hush fell on the crowd as Rose strutted to the stage where she called upon every acting trick she'd learned to make it through tonight's performance. The saloon patrons whispered, and the perpetual gamblers threw money on the table, some desperate for her to run out the door while others held their breath praying she'd stay.

Boone helped her up the two steps and whispered in her ear. "You gonna be able to do this?"

"Of course." She smiled, bowed, and waited for the piano introduction of "I Dream of Jeannie with the Light Brown Hair." The winners stuffed the money in their pockets while the losers scowled.

Through the saloon door, she watched her lover and the prostitute. When the whore fell into Callum's arms, she almost lost her mind. She continued her performance, but her attention remained transfixed on the darkness in the street. Both figures disappeared, and the Scotsman didn't return, though she willed he would during every song. When the longest performance of her life ended, she did an encore and returned to the back room to rest for her next appearance. She closed the door and held onto the wall for support. She gasped for air that would not fill her lungs, her upper body convulsed like a fish just taken from the water. She made her way to a chair and sat, air entered her lungs in short bursts.

The Scotsman had been gone long enough to…and he was…at this very moment taking his pleasure with the whore. She took deep breaths and calmed herself with the knowledge she would never belong to Callum no matter how much she wanted him. He'd asked her to marry him, told her he loved her, but she couldn't do it. The kind man deserved more than her, he deserved a family, boys to help him on the ranch and girls to sing and dance, to be the apple of his eye as she was her father's. The jealousy still hurt, and the beautiful dark-haired vixen, Amethyst, had more experience with him than she ever would. One more month of work in Wylder and she'd have enough money for her train fare to California. She'd sell her soul if she could escape tonight and not have to face Callum again.

Hoots and hollers erupted in the saloon. Rose cracked the door and peered out as Callum walked toward Russ' table. Coyote and Dalton had left, the doctor having his wife Eliza, and the gambler his firecracker Leona, waiting for them. They never stayed past the first set. Her love stood above the seated crowd with his rifle over his shoulder. His stare silenced their jeers, and everyone ventured back to the business of drinking and card playing.

Songbird eased the door shut and checked the time on her daddy's pocket watch. Thank the heavens it was almost time to go on. She waited as the first treble sounds from the piano of the Scottish song "A Red, Red Rose" rang faintly through the talk and cursing of the inebriated men. Boone placed his hands on the middle of the piano tinkling the tune with his expertise while the drunks quieted, anxious for another glimpse of their

Songbird. At the second run-through of the song, the piano player accented the bass notes, and Rose stepped into the room, let out the breath she'd held since Amethyst entered the saloon, and entertained the crowd.

Her gaze scanned over the heads of the men, not focusing on anyone and not even one glance toward Callum's table. Several times, she unclenched the fists forming at her side and forced a practiced smile to bloom on her face. The gossip mill would spill its yarn tomorrow with Widow Lowery and Eulalie Culpepper spinning the thread. Her act over, she bowed and danced to the back room through cheers and whistles. She gathered her things and prayed she'd be out the door before the Scotsman ascended from his seat and made it through the crowded saloon.

She opened the door and met the brick wall that was her lover's chest. He steadied her and escorted her from the building. A fire burned from his clasp on her arm to her heart. How dare he touch her after staying at the Social Club half the night.

When they arrived in the street away from the prying eyes of the saloon patrons, she jerked her arm free from him. "Do not touch me." Her voice escaped in a low growl. The man's chin dropped, and his shoulders slumped. An apology teased the tip of her tongue and she chided herself. What did she have to be sorry for? The words poured from her lips, and she couldn't stop them. "You're like Walker, chasing every skirt and woman's boot presented you."

Callum led her to a bench in front of the train depot. "Sit your arse down."

His large body forced her to walk backward where

she plopped down on the bench and stared up at the giant. The hurt in his eyes changed to fury. "And what do you want to say to me after you spent half the night with your whore?"

The man's temper let loose. "You women will be the death of me. I have a woman begging me to marry her and another, you to be exact, the one I love and proposed to, refuse my advances yet get jealous if you see me speak to another. Make up your mind. By all the saints in heaven, I know ye love me."

Rose caught the breath trying to escape her lungs, and her hand flew to her chest. "You arrogant Scotsman." She stood, the top of her head even with his shoulder. She shoved his chest with both hands as tears flew from her eyes. "I don't love you and I don't need you." Her fisted hands hit the hard steel of his unbending body. "I don't." Sobs racked through her, and she melted into his embrace.

Callum held the rifle over his shoulder and held her with his other arm. "*Mo chridhe*." He sat on the bench and pulled her down beside him, took her hand, and placed it on his chest. "You are my heart."

Rose gazed into his eyes. His hand held hers, and she detected a slight tremble. The Scotsman had gone from hurt to angry to afraid in a matter of a few minutes, and she was the cause. She stared at the dark ground as a raccoon paused, stared at them, and scampered away.

He put his hand under her chin and raised her face to his. "I *didnae* do anything with Amethyst but explain I loved you and had asked you to marry me. I told her I wouldn't be back even if you left town." He smoothed the red curl escaping the pins. "I am a decent man, and I talked to the woman and let my intentions be known."

Songbird's chin quivered on the verge of a tearful breakdown. He tucked his arm around her, and she rested her head on his shoulder, knowing he spoke the truth. He was honorable and kind. If things were different, if she were not barren, she'd marry him tomorrow. She planned to leave a letter to explain everything when she left Wyoming.

****

The night grew cold, dark, and lonely. Callum couldn't leave town until he was sure no one lurked in the shadows waiting to abduct his woman. The bench outside the Wylder Hotel was hard, and he longed for his bed and the warmth of his hearth.

He'd planned to stay the night, even boarded Icefall at the livery. Rose had other plans and veered away from a good-night kiss. She'd given him a curt good-bye and closed the door in his face.

The Irish redhead's temper was as explosive as the dynamite they used at the mine. Dear Christ in Heaven, he wanted to marry this woman and sire a little spark of kindling just like her. The saloon closed and the town of Wylder bedded down. He trudged toward the livery to get his horse and passed a vagrant sleeping in front of the dress shop. He recognized him as a trapper and moved on. He saddled Icefall and rode the few miles to the ranch, staring at the beauty of the stars as they blanketed the dark sky. The waning moon was just a sliver of light headed for the horizon. Life shouldn't be this complicated. He loved Rose. Rose loved him. Perhaps the lass had someone waiting for her in California. His mind raced from one scenario to another, each one more farfetched than the other.

The exhaustion from his busy day in Cheyenne and his emotional confrontation with the women made the few hours in his bed go by hard and fast. As soon as his eyes closed, sleep overcame him, but a rap on his door yanked him from his dreams. He jerked his pants on and raced to the front room in his bare feet, worried Felix had come to tell him someone had taken Rose.

He flung open the door. "Daniel, it's you. Anything wrong?" The rancher entered with a pail of milk.

"Yes, it's half-past seven. What's wrong with you? Never known you to sleep the day away. Sarah alerted me when you didn't deliver milk." He entered and closed the door behind him.

Callum hurried to his bedroom, yanked on the remainder of his clothes, and stepped into his boots. Daniel followed him to the kitchen. "Miserable night." He struck a match to light the wood stove and pumped water in the pot. He poured coffee beans into the grinder and turned the crank. "Have a seat."

Daniel gathered two cups from the wall shelf. "What happened?" He sat at the table.

"Amethyst strutted to the saloon, caused a scene, had to take her back to the Social Club. Rose was as mad as two roosters in a cock pit, wouldn't let me stay the night, so I sat on the bench outside the hotel until I was sure no one lurked about." Callum found bread and hard cheese in the cupboard. "Hungry?"

"No, just coffee." He let out a chuckle. "Bet that was a sight to see. Two women fighting over a Scotsman. I'm sure there were some wagers made on the outcome."

"Aye, and the gossip mill will be out in force after the men spread the word to the biddies in town." He poured coffee into the cups and settled down with his breakfast. "It's me own fault. I was a *dunderheid* not telling Amethyst meself. I *didnae* think it mattered. She has her life at the Social Club and other men to entertain."

Daniel sipped his coffee. "Well, Red, after you failed to court all those women who passed through town and settled in at the Social Club visiting Amethyst every week"—he placed his cup on the table and chuckled—"guess she was under the impression you cared about her as Russ cares about Miss Adelaide."

"It's different and you know it." He enjoyed his bread and cheese.

"Amethyst is in love with you, everyone in town knows." Daniel scooted his chair back and stretched his legs. "Russ loves his Addie and would marry her in nothing flat if she'd agree. Miss Adelaide Willowby cares about the welfare of her girls too much and would worry about them if she left the trade, though I know for a fact she loves Russ, too." He poured more coffee into their cups. "Amethyst, on the other hand, could be a problem."

"I took care of it last night." He stood and put his plate in the sink, then settled in his chair to finish drinking his coffee.

"Did you now?" Daniel stood, rinsed his cup, and placed it beside the plate in the sink. "Both women live in town and are bound to run up on each other. You don't think there will be words?"

"I *didnae* think of it like that." He leaned on the counter with his arms crossed. "I've got a stubborn Irish redhead with evil on her tail who refuses to marry me, a furious whore with an ax to grind wanting to marry me, and a horse ranch to run with no time to do it."

Daniel put his hand on his friend's arm. "It'll all work out, Red. I can take up the slack here. You make sure Rose is protected. Better tell Felix about Amethyst. Walker Morgan may be the least of your worries." Daniel laughed and marched out the back door.

Chapter Eleven

Rose spent a sleepless night floundering on the uncomfortable hay mattress. She got up several times to smooth the lumps in the bed and adjust her sheet. How dare Amethyst come into her place of business and make her look like a fool. And Callum, after he'd promised his undying love for only her, followed the prostitute out of the saloon like a puppy dog desperate for his mother's milk. She turned to her side and closed her eyes. A rush of discomfort rose from her stomach to her throat.

Nausea and the urge to retch tore through her body in waves. She raced to the washbowl, emptied her stomach, and held to the wooden stand until the urge passed. Her hands shook as she poured water from the pitcher into a glass and rinsed her mouth. Sweat beaded on her face, and her legs struggled to hold her in a standing position. She grasped the edge of the dresser for support and tiptoed across the cold floor to the bed. She lowered her body to the mattress and covered herself with the quilt, desperate to curl up in a ball. Sleep seized her as soon as her eyes were closed. The crow of a rooster woke her; she struggled to sit; the taste of bile lingered on her tongue. Rose sat on the bed, the floor cool beneath her feet, and waited for the dizziness to pass. A gnawing hunger replaced the nausea, and she rushed to dress and make her way downstairs to the dining room. Eulalie Culpepper had a schedule, and if you didn't arrive on time, you could forget about partaking of breakfast or supper. Rose put a biscuit and butter on her plate and poured a cup of hot tea into the chipped porcelain cup. All the boarders had eaten and left for work. The bread settled her stomach, and a renewed energy she hadn't experienced in a long time swept through her.

The sun blanketed warmth on the town of Wylder, burned off the morning fog, and dried the dew from the few blades of grass growing on the busy streets. Throughout the morning, she imagined someone following her, but the town was the same with ranchers and farmers milling through on their way to the Mercantile and the occasional drunk begging for a nickel. She touched the rosary in her pocket for luck, thankful she hadn't seen any of Morgan's henchmen. Willard Clayton was the one who terrified her. If the theater had ever needed someone to play the devil, the ex-gunslinger could fill the part.

Rose strolled to the back of the dress shop. Mary McCleary worked just inside the back door, ironing a man's shirt. "Morning, Mary."

"Good morning." The worker set the flat iron on the end of the board. "Are you all right?" She put a chair outside and peeked into the store. "Widow's gone to sleep in her chair doin' her mending." Mary placed another chair outside. "We can talk a spell."

The rumors of Mary's dead husband and his abuse mirrored her own life. In the whispered talk of the town, it was said Redmond McCleary, being drunk and distraught after a mill accident rendered his hand useless, took his own life. The gossip always reverted to Mary and her four boys and how they were treated by her husband who was supposed to protect them.

Mary worried her hands in her lap. "I heard about last night. Eulalie was in here this morning spilling it to Mildred."

"Figured as much." Rose stared at the large washtub, the water dirty from Leona's labors. Clothes filled the wires strung from the posts. "I lived with a man in Cheyenne who was not kind. I took all the blame for his actions until one day I saw him for what he was. Now, I'm embarrassed that I stayed with him as long as I did."

Mary stared at the sky. "I know how it affects a woman. Redmond still beats me in my nightmares, still yells at my boys, still runs with the whores and drunks. I pray to the Virgin Mary that someday the bad dreams will stop, and I can trust again. Trust God, trust a stranger, trust me to do what's right for my boys."

"Think you'll ever marry again?" Rose gazed at the pretty lady, thinking what a waste it would be for Mary to live her life alone after the last of her boys grew up. Everyone needed someone, didn't they?

"Me?" Mary shook her head. "No, ma'am. Don't take but one bad piece of fruit to spoil the bushel." She picked up a rock and whirled it to the edge of the yard. "I've got my friend Ruby, and my boys, and thanks to the good Lord, my job."

"Sometimes, I wonder if I'll be happy anywhere on God's green earth always glancing over my shoulder waiting for the day Walker finds me and punishes me for leaving. Men like him always seek revenge." Rose peered in the murky water in the washtub. "You're lucky Mr. McCleary can't hurt you anymore." She crossed herself. "God rest his soul."

Mary made the sign of the cross over her chest. "Yes, I pray for his sorry spirit every day, but I'm glad he isn't here to torment me and my boys. If you need to talk, I'm here, I'll listen, and I understand."

Rose rested her hand on Mary's arm. "Thank you." She walked through the passageway to Buckboard Alley and the boarding house. She climbed the few steps to the porch, stopped, and studied the street. Men and women milled in and out of stores, but no one caught her eye. She woke every day with the knowledge Walker would send a search party. Wylder wasn't far enough away from Cheyenne, no place was, although he didn't have connections here as he did in Denver.

A basket of clean clothes sat beside the entrance to her room. She glanced around the dim hallway and unlocked her door, stuck her head in the room to check that her space had not been disturbed, and picked up the basket of clothes. Rose secured the door and went to the task of tidying her rented room. She placed the clean clothes in her trunk and smoothed the sheets and quilt on her bed. A knock on her door and the rattle of the doorknob halted her movements. The floorboards in her room creaked when walked on, so she froze and waited for the departure of their footsteps.

"I know you're in there." A harder knock. "It's Amethyst. I want to talk to you."

Rose had no desire to see the woman, as soon as she left for California, Callum would pick up his affair with the prostitute and she'd be forgotten like last fall's leaves. Songbird opened the door a small way and rested her foot against it. "What do you want?"

Amethyst shoved her way inside. Rose tripped on the hem of her dress and landed on the bed with a plop.

The prostitute sat. "I have a few things to say to you and I'll be on my way. First, Callum is mine, not yours. He thinks he loves you, but you're just another of his conquests. You ain't the first pair of legs to drift into this town he's chased, and you won't be the last. Difference is, I stay, and you won't. We're no different, me and you. I may be a whore, but you're a saloon singer who lived out of wedlock for years." She smiled and puffed her chest out. "Everybody in town knows your business." She smoothed her hair under her hat. "Yes ma'am, ain't no difference, both of us earning our living on our backs."

Rose's spine straightened and her palm collided with the side of Amethyst's face. Her hand burned from the contact and her body trembled with anger. "Get out of my room." Her voice resonated in her ears as if it belonged to another person. She opened the door and stepped back to give the whore space to exit. Rose's eyes gazed into the made-up eyes of the prostitute. "I feel sorry for you. You think a man loves you because he visits you every week giving you a poke to ease his wants. What about the rest of the time when he's out living his life, if he cared for you as you say, you'd be beside him as his wife not his Saturday harlot." Rose forced the woman out, slammed the door, and opened her window to let the hussy's perfume escape on the wind.

Desperate to get away from the gossip of the town, Rose dressed in her riding skirt and hurried to the livery. She needed to be with her horse and feel the breeze spiral through her hair and weave its way into her brain to settle the cyclone that had whirled since the day Callum rescued her. Damn the Scotsman, for making her feel, for making her care, for making her love.

She'd forget him as soon as she got to California, and he could get back to his visits to the Wylder County Social Club. She waved to Russ Holt and smiled; this was the second time today she'd seen him. Unusual for him to be in town this early unless he was visiting Miss Addie.

Chet worked to shoe a horse she'd not seen before. He released the animal's leg and wiped his hands on his apron. "Good day, Miss O'Brien. Going for a ride?"

"Yes, won't be gone long, need to ride Daisy so she doesn't forget who I am." Rose entered the stalls, followed by Chet.

"Let me help you." Chet retrieved her saddle and readied the Palomino. "Cinch secure and all is ready."

Rose led the horse to the street and mounted the mare. "Thanks, Mr. Daniels." She adjusted the reins and directed the horse out of town.

She spurred Daisy to a slow trot on Old Cheyenne Road and became one with the horse, her worries dissipated, and her breathing slowed. The mare sensed the calm and slowed to a walk, plodding along the dirt road. Rose rubbed the horse's neck and talked, giving the horse all the reasons she had to leave Wylder and Callum behind, her fears of Walker Morgan, and her promise to pay the horse's train fare to California. Daisy let out a loud whinny, she laughed and spurred the animal to a fast gallop. Both needed freedom from being jailed, she in her rented room and her pet in the small stall at the livery. They drifted almost as far as the

Lex Taylor Ranch and made a U-turn.

An old man dressed in dirty clothes and an old hat approached, riding a mule. He tipped his hat. "Ma'am."

"Afternoon," Rose responded, feeling alone and exposed. She spurred Daisy to a gallop and hurried back to town.

Chet wasn't in the livery, so she unsaddled the horse and put everything in the storage room. She walked down Old Cheyenne Road, where she found Boone Layton sitting on a bench outside the Five Star Saloon. "Boone."

The piano player patted the seat beside him. "Take a load off your feet."

She sat and clasped her hands in her lap. "Thanks, Boone." People meandered down the street, and she recognized the man she'd seen on the road. She nodded her head toward him. "I met him on the road heading out of town on a mule."

Boone rested his hat in his lap and wiped the sweat off his brow. "Riding a mule, you say? Must be a miner, forgot something and returned."

"Glad I ran into you." Rose nodded to one of the regulars as he entered the saloon. "I'm leaving in a month for San Francisco."

Boone faced her. "A month? You just got here. Our act is making money. Sonny said if it continued, he'd raise our pay."

She gazed into the dark eyes of her friend. "Go with me, Boone. You don't have anything here, and with your talent, you'd have more work than you can do."

He breathed deep and sent his gaze above the roof of the rail office. "Well, you're right about nothing to hold me here. Emerald is a fine lady, with caramel skin and green eyes. I thought I'd rescue her and take her to a new town, start a new life for us both." His voice grew quiet, and he whispered, "I get the sneaky suspicion she and Abraham would like to be a pair if they could." He lifted his head and rubbed his chin. "When I first got to Wylder, I visited her quite a bit, until I couldn't take the way that huge man glared at me as if I abused his girl, and me a paying customer."

"Might be the small town and everyone familiar with the goings-on, but it seems the whore house has a mind of its own. I've got Amethyst demanding I leave her man alone, and you've got Abraham the bouncer jealous of you, a paying client." Rose bent to tie her bootlace; the action caused her stomach to let out a loud growl. "Sorry, I had lunch already, don't know why my stomach is rumbling."

"Better get something to eat before your show tonight." He stood. "I'll escort you wherever it is you're heading."

"To my room. But guess I need to stop at Jake's Place." They turned right on Sidewinder Lane. "Let's start our performance with "The Rose of Allandale" tonight."

Boone nodded his head. "Good choice. I'll write out the order and leave it for you."

She stopped in front of the restaurant. "Thanks, Boone, see you tonight."

After a quick meal, Rose returned to the boarding house. Eulalie supervised a young girl as she cleaned the floor of the dining room. Her cruel words when the girl didn't scrub to her liking made Rose cringe. She said a silent prayer for the young woman and climbed the stairs to her room.

Rose removed her dress and sat in a chair wearing her chemise and pantaloons and enjoyed the strong breeze that swept through the window. Her urge to leave Wylder and her love for Callum clashed and thwarted her reasoning. The longer she stayed in Wylder the stronger her love for the Scotsman grew. To leave him would fracture her heart like a porcelain vase that could never be mended. But, to stay she would disappoint him. Her love for Callum MacPhilip was too strong to allow that to happen. She relaxed until the food settled in her stomach and took another walk around town.

Chapter Twelve

Callum arrived in Wylder late morning after a few grueling hours helping Daniel fix the broken axle on Sarah's carriage. The job couldn't wait—Sarah grew bigger every day and Daniel didn't want to chance not having proper transportation in case he had to take her to town for the birth.

On his way to Wylder, he contemplated kidnapping Songbird himself and forcibly depositing her in the church where the priest could marry them. Problem solved. He'd have the woman he loved, and she'd be protected from Morgan and his men. Damn, the stubborn woman.

He hid in the shadows as Songbird flitted around town. She'd spent a good hour at the dress shop, then went to her room at the boarding house. Callum entered Jake's Place and sat at a window table. The midmorning business was slow, so Jake joined him and poured each a cup of coffee. The men enjoyed the hot brew and talked about horses, town gossip, and recipes when Rose stormed down the walk like the demons of hell were after her. Her riding skirt was the clue he needed. He paid and made his way to the corner of Sidewinder Lane and Old Cheyenne Road and stuck his head around the corner. As suspected, she headed to the livery.

"*Shite.*" He ran to his horse. He'd forgotten about

her riding habit. He prayed the lass would take her usual route. He mounted his quarter horse and raced away from town to find a place to hide and watch. They entered a stand of trees, and he tied his ride far enough away from the road where she wouldn't hear or see his horse. Callum hid among the cedars and waited.

Rose and Daisy galloped past him. Several yards behind, an old man and a mule headed out of town. It was Felix Ross, the Pinkerton detective. A few moments later, Songbird had Daisy in a canter going back to town. Callum retrieved Finlay and they entered the road as Felix passed by headed back to Wylder.

Callum rode up beside the mule. "Almost didn't recognize you." He stared at the pack mule and laughed. "That's a sorry animal for surveillance. What if you had to rescue her from the bad men?"

Mr. Ross rubbed the sweat off his brow with his shirt sleeve. "Chet Daniels had the horseshoes off my mustang and this was all he had. Why didn't you tell me she had a horse?"

"I didn't think of it." He kept Finlay walking at the mule's pace. "Anything suspicious going on?"

Felix bounced and clicked his tongue to get the animal to speed up. "Nothing except a catfight with a prostitute this morning. I followed Miss O'Brien into the boarding house. Made my way to her floor and had to duck into a vacant room because a beautiful painted lady knocked on her door. She refused to let the woman enter but the whore bullied her way inside, where they had words. Seems you've got two women squabbling over you."

"*Shite*, I'll be a donkey's arse. I told Amethyst I didn't care about her, but she won't leave it be." His blood heated in his veins. Rose's safety was his top priority, and now Amethyst and her jealousy would drive his woman to another town further away from him.

"Anything else I should know?" The detective dug his feet into the side of the mule and clicked his tongue.

"No." Callum stewed and vowed never to speak to Amethyst again. Reasoning with a hellcat would get him torn to shreds. "You go on ahead and I'll take a back way into town."

He tugged the reins and stopped Finlay in the middle of Old Cheyenne Road, giving the slow mule time to get ahead of him, and veered right to enter the town by way of Wylder Street. All he wanted to do was strong-arm Walker Morgan, beat the *shite* out of him, and make him promise to leave Rose alone. But rich men were a breed of their own in the west. The man's wealth didn't come from a small theater in Cheyenne, of that he was certain. If the lass would marry him, say yes to his request, listen to reason, their problems would be solved. She loved him. He was more sure of that than his name was Callum MacPhilip. All Irish women were stubborn, it was bred into them. However, this redhead had to be a mix of Scottish and Irish with some English aristocracy thrown in.

He tied his horse to the hitching post in front of the McCabe and McClain Law Office, confident Rose wouldn't venture this far. Russ Holt rested on a bench outside the sheriff's office. The Scotsman whistled to get his attention and motioned for him to join him in the alley between the law office and the bank.

Russ crossed the street after a wagon with two young boys hanging on the back passed. "Callum, haven't seen you all day. Figured you'd be in town by now seeing after your lady."

Callum searched the area to make sure they weren't followed. "I've been here a while. Rose decided to ride Daisy, and I was out on Old Cheyenne Road. Have you seen anything out of the ordinary?"

Russ leaned against the side of the bank building. "I've been here all day. Seen our girl three times."

"Did she see you?" The Scotsman put his hands on his hips.

"Twice, she smiled and waved, don't think she saw me the third time. Does it matter?" Russ propped his foot on a large rock.

"Yes, it matters." He crossed his arms and stared at the older man "We don't want her to know we're watching her. Can you be more discreet?"

"Discreet, you say? Well, I guess you didn't hear about this." Russ lowered his voice and glanced to both ends of the street. "I was in the Social Club this morning with Miss Addie, and we were in her room, you know, visitin', and I overheard Amethyst talking to Emerald in the hall. Seems your Miss Amethyst had a confrontation with Rose at the boarding house and your Wylder Rose slapped Amethyst in the face."

"Holy *shite*, she *skelped* her?" Callum paced back and forth. If he could beat everyone's arse causing trouble starting with the prostitute and ending with Walker Morgan, then give the Songbird a good spanking, he'd have this cleared up in no time. "This is what you are going to do since you aren't good at surveillance. You're in charge of Amethyst. If she comes in the saloon, approaches me on the street, or approaches Rose anywhere, you take care of it."

Russ lifted his hat and scratched his head. "How?"

He stepped close to Russ and spoke in a low voice. "You've been at the Social Club more than anyone in town. You should know by now how to handle these women. Handle it."

Russ placed his hat on his head. "I'll take care of the situation." He peered to his left and nodded his head toward Wylder Street.

The Scotsman's eyes met Rose's glare. Their gazes locked while he addressed his friend. "See you tonight at the saloon, Russ."

"Yep." Russ shuffled toward Old Cheyenne Road.

Callum advanced toward his woman like she was a wild horse. Afraid she would bolt, he put out his hand as he inched toward her. "Rose, me love."

She straightened her spine and crossed her arms over her chest. "And what were you two doing hiding in the alley? Did you give him a secret message for your precious gemstone?"

He stopped in front of her, desperate to take her in his arms and race to the boarding house and love her as he did in his cabin. In her mood, she'd have him arrested. "Jesus, Mary, and Joseph, woman. What does it take for you to believe me? You are the woman I love." Frustration boiled over like water in a tea kettle. "You are the most stubborn, pig-headed, independent…" A tear dripped from her left eye. He cradled her face in his hands. "Beautiful, amazing, talented woman I've ever known, and I love you, lass." She relaxed against his chest, finding the spot her head always slid to. He held her as people shuffled around them, staring as they passed. "I'm your man, Rose. Please don't fight me."

She backed away. "Seems I go from one problem in Cheyenne to multiple complications in Wylder, and I've not been well today."

He checked her forehead for fever and put his hands on the sides of her face. "Let's find Doc Sullivan."

"No, no, I'm out of sorts is all." She smoothed the skirt of her dress. "I need to rest before tonight. You can accompany me to my room."

He tucked his hand around her waist and led her to Culpepper's. Felix Ross had changed into a suit with a vest and tie and leaned against the post in front of the Wylder Hotel. Callum cut his eyes toward the man and gave him a silent back-off stare. Felix wandered into the hotel, and they strolled to the boarding house.

She dug through her reticule for the key. "Thanks for accompanying me. I'll be fine."

He entered the room with her, where she sat on the bed and removed her boots and stockings. "Lay back and rest. I'm gonna be right here." Covering her with a sheet, he settled in the chair.

She snuggled on her pillow. "Wake me at seven."

Callum checked his watch for the fifth time since she'd been resting. Rose had slept the two hours away as deep as she did after he'd rescued her from the snow. Five minutes after seven. He placed a kiss on her cheek. "Time to get up, love."

She stretched and rubbed her eyes. "Have you been here the entire time?"

"Aye." He drew her in his arms. "I'll leave you to get ready and I'll be waiting outside on the porch to escort you." He slipped out the door and bounded down the stairs. Eulalie Culpepper stood at the desk with a sour expression on her face. "Miss Eulalie." He tipped his hat and lumbered outside.

****

Rose slipped on her most comfortable dress, teal silk with lace sleeves. Her queasy stomach and the weariness from the day's excitement troubled her. She didn't like to perform ill, but the show must go on. She donned her jewelry and picked up the perfume bottle but the remembrance of the smell on her skin made her stomach roil. A belch escaped her throat and she put her hand on her chest and swallowed. She reached for her shawl and gazed around the room to make sure she had everything she needed for her performance.

As they entered the saloon, the clientele stopped their card games and a hush fell over the room. Patrick O'Donnell, owner of the mine and her best supporter, stood and clapped, the other men followed suit. The older man hadn't missed any of her shows and shouted out requests for his favorite Irish songs every night. She nodded toward him and smiled. "Evening, Mr. O'Donnell."

"Ma'am," he said as he sat and settled to his poker game.

Rose paced around the small room. Her life had unraveled years ago, and she'd coped pouring her heart into her music and acting. The worry over her health was disconcerting and foreign. She'd never had more than a sniffle, always careful to avoid drafts and take care of her throat, drinking hot tea and chewing peppermint leaves. If her sick stomach didn't clear up in a few days, she would see Doc Sullivan. Boone played her traveling music. She said a quick prayer before opening the door and sashaying to the stage.

Most of the men stood at her entrance and again after the performance. She blew kisses to the kind audience, grateful there were still men who treated a lady with respect even if she was just a saloon singer.

Callum sat in his usual spot with Russ Holt, and she flashed a smile in his direction. The Scotsman seemed on edge today, and the thought of telling him she would soon depart Wylder caused a hollow ache in her lower stomach. He'd been so kind, kinder than any man had ever been in her life, and she loved him. He deserved an explanation and not a letter or note. She would tell him soon.

She sang the second verse of "Camptown Races" and the men were still clapping and talking when Amethyst stalked into the saloon and made her way straight to the Scotsman's table. She continued to sing, but her legs wanted to run off the stage and her hands tensed wanting to grab the woman and kick her out the door when Russ Holt escorted the harlot from the saloon. Callum never acknowledged the woman was there. His gaze focused on her.

The show over, they strolled to Culpepper's Boarding House with Callum's protective hand around her waist. His rifle rested on his shoulder held by his other hand. The man gave her a sense of security, something she'd not had since bedding with Walker Morgan. Would she ever forget the nightmare?

He unlocked the door and stepped inside with her. "May I kiss you goodnight?" He placed his rifle on the bed.

"You may." His lips met hers with gentle short kisses. He held her so close, she could breathe in the essence of him. He deepened the kiss, and her body betrayed her, craving everything he could give. To her surprise, he released her and retrieved his gun.

Callum paused at the door. "Get some rest, *mo ghràdh*. I *ken* you still aren't well; your color is pale, and your eyes lack the usual brightness." He lifted her chin, so her eyes gazed into his. "I love you, lass. You are my woman whether you will admit it or not. And I am your man."

Chapter Thirteen

Rose woke to a loud boom and a flash of lightning streaking the sky outside her window. The strong breeze thrust the downpour of cold rain through her room; the mist settled on her skin and dampened the sheet. She jumped out of bed and closed the window. The sudden action made her dizzy, and she used the wall as support to get to the washbowl. Aware most stomach ailments were caused by worry made her determination to get to San Francisco even stronger. She splashed water on her face, dressed in a plain cotton dress and boots, and made her way to the dining room.

Eulalie Culpepper fussed around the table, pouring fresh coffee in cups. "Take a seat."

Rose sat at the table and glanced at the boarders devouring their breakfast. She sipped the freshly brewed liquid. Eggs, sausage, and bread on a thick white plate were placed before her. She sampled the eggs and swallowed, cleared her throat, and willed the food to stay put. She cut a piece of meat and raised it to her mouth; the smell made her stomach churn. The dry biscuit and coffee were the only things that appeared appetizing. A loud boom shook the two-story house to its foundation. Her body jerked from the sound and coffee spilled from the cup she held in her hand onto the wooden table.

"Silly girl," Eulalie scolded as she wiped up the hot liquid. "What's the matter with you? It's just a storm." She scurried to the kitchen to make more coffee.

The boarders trudged their way into the rainy morning, leaving Rose alone. Her coffee had grown cold, so she nibbled on the bread.

Miss Culpepper entered the room. "You don't look well." She sat in a chair and stared at Rose. "You have morning sickness. You know what that means. Serves you right for whoring around." She laughed and cleared the table of plates and cups. "He won't marry you."

"It's not what you think. Callum is a good man. You're a rude, mean, old woman." The words escaped her lips, and she wouldn't apologize, she meant every word and more. The busybody left the room and returned with a cup of hot water and a piece of ginger floating in it.

Eulalie placed the cup before her. "Here. Can't stand to see anyone sick." She exhaled a disgusted sigh and left the dining room.

Rose sipped the herbal concoction and her stomach settled. The busybody was wrong. She was thirty years old and had accepted the fact she was barren after many years of praying otherwise. She'd get her health back when she left the West behind and started her new life in California.

The spring thunderstorm blew in the last cold air of winter. Rose rested in her room covered in a quilt until the rain stopped before she ventured outside.

Clouds rolled above, revealing a blue sky, then circled again to darken the afternoon. She stepped around mud holes on her way to the livery to check on Daisy. Rose presented the mare with a carrot and commenced brushing and grooming. She hummed to calm her pet, who'd never taken to storms of any kind. With the grooming done, she closed the gate and stood with her arms over the rail until Daisy sauntered to the other side of the stall and stuck her head outside the window. The town was quiet, and there were few people on the street as she exited the livery to find lunch, surprised she was ravenous for food after being so ill this morning. She walked up the alley toward the Catholic church.

"Turn around and walk," the gunslinger growled.

Willard Clayton's voice sent chills down her spine and the cold nozzle of his six-gun bore into Rose's back. The muscles in her body tensed, fear caused an ache in her chest, and her dry throat made the involuntary action to swallow impossible. "I'm not going back." Her voice spoke with more confidence than she had. Her body jerked as he dug the cold end of his revolver against her back. She bolted, her long skirt tangled around her legs as she raced toward Wylder Street and the sheriff's office.

A hand grabbed her arm and swung her around. "Don't go back, but you'll die here in this piss-ant town, and I'll carry your body to Mr. Morgan. He wants you in Cheyenne, dead or alive." He spat on the sidewalk. "I've never killed a woman. You'll be my first."

His fingers dug into her arm while searing pain radiated to her hand. She stared into his cold eyes. "Kill me, you bastard. Shoot me dead. I don't care anymore."

Willard forced her toward the large black carriage and opened the door. "After I kill you, he's next."

Rose inhaled a ragged breath and stared at Homer

117

Adams. His hands were tied in his lap while blood dripped down his face from a cut below his eye. His head rested on the back of the seat. Holy Virgin Mary, please let him be alive, she prayed. Terrified for him and his wife Bessie, she stepped into the seat beside him.

Clayton placed his gun in the holster and tied her hands with rope. "After the master gets through with you, you won't be runnin' off again." He slammed the door and whistled as the carriage shifted from his weight when he climbed to the driver's seat and guided the horses out of town.

Rose elbowed Mr. Adams. "Homer, are you all right? Please wake up."

Mr. Adams stirred and jerked upright. He spat blood on the floor of the carriage and faced her. "My dear, I'm so sorry. Bessie and I should have left. He is Lucifer's spawn hurting innocent women and paying thieves and gunmen to rob the train."

She wanted to see to Homer's injuries, but her hands were bound so tight her fingers were growing numb from lack of blood. "I've regretted leaving you and Bessie in Cheyenne, but I got caught in the snowstorm and almost met my end on Old Cheyenne Road. You would both have died then."

"I know about the man who rescued you. Mr. MacPhilip visited the house and told us you were fine, and he watched out for you." Mr. Adams twisted his hands to loosen the rope.

"Callum went to Cheyenne?" Hope swelled her heart that he would come. "When was this?"

"A few weeks past." He gave her a kind smile. "He's our only hope now."

Rose couldn't remember if there was anyone around the church or in the back alley when she left the livery. Callum wouldn't know until he arrived in town and found her gone. But what if Boone told him she'd gone to San Francisco by way of Denver, and they assumed she'd left? It would take days for them to realize her things were still in her room. She wrung her wrists to loosen the rope, which caused more pain on her tender skin. She let her body fall against the back of the seat and planned how to keep Homer and Bessie safe.

The carriage slowed, then stopped. The door opened and Willard hauled her out, tripping her with his foot. She fell into the soft, muddy earth. He jerked the old man out and threw him against the side of the buggy. Rose wallowed in the mud while her tied hands sank into the earth. She rolled to her back for the leverage she needed to raise her body to a sitting position and stood. Her boots mired into the water and mud. "Don't hurt him." She wobbled toward the gunslinger.

Clayton drew both his guns and pointed them at their heads. "Get in the house."

Mr. Morgan stepped on the porch. "Appears the kitten gave you some trouble."

"Nothing I couldn't handle." Willard put his guns in their holster.

Walker held a knife in his hand. "You aren't coming into my house with mud and filth on you. Take off your clothes. All of them." He cut the ropes from her hands and did the same for Homer Adams.

Rose glanced at the three men; a tear dripped from Homer's eye. She unlaced her boots and tugged them off, her stockinged feet absorbed the cold from the wooden stoop. Her mud-soaked dress clung to her body and the buttons were difficult to manage with her stiff fingers. She peeled the dress off and threw it on the ground. The muddy and wet chemise and bloomers hugged the curves of her body. A primal guttural groan escaped from Willard, and she stepped back and wrapped her hands around her middle.

"I said all of them." Walker grabbed her chemise and ribbed the bodice from her body. "Step out of those pantaloons or I'll take them off for you."

The cold damp air fell over Rose's naked breasts, making her nipples grow hard, and chill bumps raked over her skin as her face heated in embarrassment. Angry but defiant, her confidence assured her this devil would not win. Homer closed his eyes, but Willard's lascivious stare, the bulge rising in his pants and his hand that inched toward her made her follow her captor's orders. She stepped out of her bloomers and glared at Walker Morgan.

She'd lived with the extent of Walker's vicious ways a long time, but the hatred and lust from the younger man scared her in ways her former lover never could.

Walker criticized everything she did, her singing, the way she ate or didn't eat her food, the way she dressed, her hair, her body. He'd done whatever he could to control her and break her spirit, but her faith and the knowledge good always won over evil gave her the strength to leave him, and she would again. This time with her friends.

Walker Morgan brandished his knife toward Willard. "Don't go getting any ideas. She belongs to me." He stared at his henchman until the gunslinger nodded in agreement. "If anyone comes, kill 'em."

Homer faced Morgan. "Where's my wife?"

Mr. Morgan opened the back door. "Don't worry, old man, Bessie's waiting for you in Rose's bedroom." They entered through the kitchen and headed to the front foyer and the stairs. He held his knife to Homer's back as they ascended the steps. "Get in there." He opened the door for the old man and put the knife in his pocket.

Walker ran his hand through Rose's hair and whispered in her ear. "You are mine. I made you who you are. You owe everything you are to me." He rested his hand on her ass and positioned his body close.

She broke free, her spine stiffened, and she stood straight and proud. "I will never be yours and I owe you nothing."

He opened the knife and positioned it against her neck. "I'd love to cut your throat and watch you bleed, but I need you to sing at the theater. Business is down since you left." He opened the door to the room and nudged her inside. "Get some clothes on." He threw his head back and laughed. "Songbird."

Bessie grabbed a quilt from the bed and draped it around Rose. "What did he do to you?" She led the girl to the bowl and pitcher and poured water on a cloth. "How did you get so filthy?"

She stood before the old woman like a child. "I fell in the yard and Walker made me take off my muddy clothes before entering the house."

She wiped the dirt and grime from Rose's face. "He's done the most appalling things since you've been gone, but this is the worst." She sat her in a chair and combed the caked mud from her hair. "You're shivering."

The lady addressed her husband, who studied the wallpaper. "Homer, for goodness' sake, you've seen a naked woman before. Light the fire and some lamps." Bessie rummaged through drawers for underwear and rushed to the large trunk for a dress.

Homer lit the kindling, which brought the fire to life. Rose could feel the heat from the hearth and the warmth of the clothes as the older lady dressed her. "Thank you, Bessie, I'm so sorry I left you both here."

"Shhh." The lady buttoned the dress and eased the girl back to the chair. "No one held a gun to our head. We didn't have any place else to go. The master's lost his mind and now we'll live on the street if we must." She brushed the long wavy locks. "I'm sorry he found you. We hoped you'd marry that nice Scottish fellow. I saw him from the window. Handsome, he is."

Callum—she prayed he would come but she prayed he'd stay away. They would kill him, and she couldn't live with herself if they did. Best if he believed she fled to Denver.

The old woman plodded toward the door. "I'm going downstairs to make us some tea and see what's in the larder."

"No." Rose tugged Bessie to her side.

The lady squeezed Rose's hand. "I'm not a threat, he won't hurt me." She crossed the floor. "Homer, stay with her."

She sat in the chair the old man placed in front of the fireplace. "Please sit, Mr. Adams. It's going to be a long night."

Homer sat in a straight chair opposite Rose. "We'll

all escape next time."

She stared into the fire. "I promise I won't leave without you and Bessie."

The housekeeper entered the room with hot tea, bread, cheese, and sweet biscuits. "This is all I could find."

Rose devoured the meager portions. "Where's Walker?"

Bessie poured more tea into Rose's cup. "He's in his office, drinking whiskey." She made a tent with her index fingers and placed them over her lips, while a smile bloomed on her face. "I put a sleeping powder in his bottle after he gave orders to Mr. Clayton this afternoon." She put more cheese on each plate. "I peeked in his room and he's asleep on the settee."

Rose closed her eyes and breathed a sigh of relief. The old woman had bought them time. "Who else is guarding the house?"

The lady sipped her tea. "Sam's hiding out in front and Willard's watching the back."

"I'll return in a few moments." Rose hurried to leave.

Homer followed her. "I'll come with you."

"No." She gave him a stern stare. "I won't be long, going to check on Walker and get his gun."

"Lord, girl. Be careful." He entered the hall and watched as she slipped down the stairs.

Rose stopped in the foyer, listening for anyone in the house. She eased into Walker's sitting room and crossed the floor to his desk. She pulled out drawers as quietly as she could until she found his revolver.

Rose lifted the heavy pistol, crossed the floor, and picked up his knife resting on the side table. Her eyes swept over her tormentor. His body reclined on the settee; his hand rested on the floor with the glass a few inches away.

Advancing years had not been his friend. His balding head made him appear much older than his forty-five years and the hair he had left was gray. She searched her heart for any love and her brain for one happy memory of her time here but found neither. Bessie and Homer fussed over her and treated her like their daughter, but even they had to turn a blind eye to the mistreatment. She climbed the stairs, planning their escape.

Chapter Fourteen

The spring storm disrupted Callum's workday. First, the rain and wind kept him and Daniel in their respective homes, and after it subsided, the ground was so muddy they struggled to hike the paths to the barn and chicken coop. It was midmorning when the chores were done, and Callum had to strip off his clothes and wash the mud off his body before heading to Wylder.

He met up with Doctor Coyote Sullivan and Russ at the saloon. "Anyone seen Rose today?"

Russ sipped a cup of coffee. "Chet said she came by after the storm to sit with her horse, but he had to go to the Mercantile and didn't see her leave."

Coyote leaned on the table. "I haven't seen her today, but most people are staying in because of the muddy streets."

A wave of fear crashed against Callum's spine; the foreboding sent a cold sweat that collected in his belly and darted to his heart in an accelerated rush. "Anyone seen Felix Ross today?"

Russ walked to the counter to get more coffee. "Yep, this morning outside the hotel."

Seamus and Peter McCleary entered the saloon and looked around. "Mr. MacPhilip?" Seamus called out.

Callum hurried to the entrance. "What do ye boys need?"

Peter gazed up at the ceiling and down to the floor

of the saloon, taking in the entire room while his older brother passed the message from their mother. "Ma wanted us to find ya and tell ya that Malachy and Daniel was playin' in the mud today and seen a man push Rose in his carriage. They run after the buggy, but it was a big un an' had two horses, they couldn't keep up." Seamus took a deep breath and stared at the Scotsman.

Callum's heartbeat sounded in his ears like a steady drumbeat keeping time to a slow dirge. One he would sing when he killed the person responsible. "Which way did they go?" He grabbed Seamus's arms.

"Toward Cheyenne." The boy backed up. "Ma said you'd be upset."

The Scotsman grabbed his rifle. "Tell your Ma I appreciate the information and I'm thankful her youngest was out this morning." The boys stood stock still taking in every inch of the saloon. He pulled coins from his pocket and gave one to each boy. "Go on with yourselves and tell your Ma I'll get Rose back to Wylder."

After the boys left the saloon, he addressed Coyote and Russ. "You can tell the sheriff if you want, but I don't think he'll have any jurisdiction on this, and if you see Felix Ross let him know." He placed his hat on his head.

Russ halted him. "Don't want to cause any ire, but what if she went on her own accord? Hell, she couldn't be happy in Wylder. Her coming from Cheyenne with an acting and singing career to perform in a saloon with drunks, cowboys, and gamblers." He backed away from the Scotsman. "And, let me say this. You said she'd been with Mr. Morgan for years, maybe she wanted to go back."

Callum paused and let his unspoken fear penetrate his brain. He'd contemplated over the reason she refused to marry him for days. It could be she still loved the bastard. He uttered the most difficult words he ever spoke. "If that's the case, I'll let her be."

Russ grabbed his hat. "I'll go with you, then."

Coyote checked the bullets in his revolver. "I volunteer my assistance."

"Aye, appreciate it." Callum rested his rifle on his shoulder. "Let's ride."

Sonny approached. "You men be careful. I'll see to the sheriff and detective."

Doc Sullivan spoke to the bartender. "Send word to Eliza. Tell her not to worry, I'll be home as soon as this business is done."

"Will do." Sonny cleared their table of glasses and cups and deposited them onto the bar.

The men rode their steeds hard and fast to Cheyenne. Callum's heart told him she didn't want to go back to her old life, but his intellect toyed with the truth Russ could be correct in his thinking. Rose had stayed with the man ten years, she must have loved him and could still, though he would have to hear the declaration from her lips.

Lamplight delivered a hazy illumination as they entered the town of Cheyenne and stopped three streets away from Morgan's home in front of a business. Each man dismounted and tied the reins to a post, letting the horses drink water from the trough. "Here's what we'll do." Callum checked the bullets in his pistol. "Leave the horses here. If they took her against her will, he'll have lookouts posted. If there are none, I'll demand answers."

Doc Sullivan interrupted. "If they have guards, let me get in the house first and you two take them out."

"No, I'm going in the house to rescue her." The Scotsman retrieved his rifle from the scabbard.

"Callum." Coyote blocked his path. "I can get in there with no one seeing me, you're much bigger and somewhat bullish if you don't mind me saying. Let's use the talents God gave us to save the woman."

"Aye." Callum ran the scenario in his head. "Ye be right."

In the cloak of darkness, the men made their way to the mansion. The Scotsman stopped, the men following suit. "I see one in the front. He's to the right, leaned against the wall in the middle of the house."

"See him." Russ put his hand on the pistol resting in his belt. "I can take him."

"I'll check the sides of the house and the back." Callum nodded to Coyote. "Do your magic and get in the house."

Coyote wandered off and Callum searched the darkness for his friend, one minute he walked beside them, and the next he'd disappeared. "Give me time to check out the sides and back. At my whistle, take him down."

Russ plucked his gun from the holster. "My apology. Guess she didn't go of her own accord. Let's get her back."

He put his hand on Russ's shoulder. "Be careful, don't want Miss Addie's wrath upon me if you get hurt."

"I've still got some fight left in me." Russ strode left and Callum positioned himself behind the house.

He recognized Willard Clayton standing at the back door but found no one lurking on the side. He would be happy to take this man out. He left his rifle propped against the house and made the sound of a hoot owl. He waited until Clayton advanced in the opposite direction from him and approached using the butt of his pistol to knock the guard out. He took the man's pistols, grabbed his rifle, and checked out the other side of the house before wandering to the front. Russ wrestled with a younger man, holding him around the neck in an arm hold. Callum approached and punched the guard in the face, knocking him out cold, and retrieved his gun. "That's all I've seen, let's get inside." He passed one pistol to Russ and tucked the other two in his belt.

He pounded the locked knob with the butt of his revolver and entered the dark house. He and Russ split up and searched through the bottom floor. He entered the room with a glowing light and found the owner passed out on the settee. As he rounded the corner to the stairs, Coyote appeared.

"They're up here." Doc waited while he ascended the stairs.

"Russ," Callum shouted.

Holt entered the foyer. "Didn't see anyone."

Callum nodded toward the front room. "Appears he's sleeping off a bender. Watch him while I get Rose." He ascended the stairs three at a time and followed Doc Sullivan to a room at the far end of the dimly lit hallway. Songbird hurried to his arms. He cradled her with one arm while holding the rifle in his other hand. His heart thumped a steady relief—the sound filled his ears as her scent filled his lungs. "Thank God you're all right." The older couple sat together on the side of the bed. "You folks be okay?"

Homer nodded toward his wife. "We are now."

Heavy footsteps and shouts filled the bottom floor of the mansion.

Doc Sullivan raced to the door. "I'll check it out."

They waited several minutes and listened to a discussion from below. Coyote entered the room with Russ and Felix Ross.

Felix nodded his head. "Evening, everyone. Glad you're all safe. We've got the men in custody downstairs."

Callum wanted to kill Ross for not seeing to Rose's safety. "I paid you to take care of the lass and I'm the one who rescued her. Where have you been all this time?"

Felix Ross stood tall and replied, "There has been an ongoing investigation in the horrendous dealings of Mr. Morgan and his henchmen. I had to get my detectives together along with the sheriff and deputy to apprehend them. We had everything under control."

"Well, I'm glad you did, seeing we were the ones who did your work for you." Russ holstered his gun. "Guess it was easy arresting men who were already knocked out."

Doc Sullivan smiled at the captors. "Which one of you put a sleeping powder in the man's drink?"

Bessie raised her hand. "That'd be me." She gave them a bright smile. "I may be old, but I'm still devious."

"How'd you know?" Callum asked. "He appeared drunk to me."

"I checked him out, didn't want any trouble from him but didn't want to harm him either. Hippocratic oath." Coyote tipped his hat and smiled.

The rumble of men's voices soared through the night air. Callum opened the window and peered into the darkness. He recognized saloon patrons from Wylder holding torches and chanting. "Songbird. We want Songbird. Songbird. We want Songbird." The sound floated on the wind into the open window.

Boone Layton raced into the room. "Rose." He hesitated and stared at the room full of people. "Thank God."

"I'm fine, Boone." She put her hand on his arm. "He didn't hurt me."

"I was so worried about you." The piano player stood with his hat in his hand. "The men at the saloon found out and hightailed it over here. If these three hadn't rescued you, they were going to."

She placed her hand on Boone's cheek. "How kind of them and you, too. You've been my best friend through this." She smiled at Homer and Bessie. "I don't know what I would have done without the three of you."

The sheriff entered the room. "Gentlemen, ladies." He addressed Rose, Homer, and Bessie. "You folks aren't hurt, are you?"

Rose spoke up. "No, sir. We're fine."

"Better have the bruise on your face seen about." After her nod, he continued. "The perpetrators are being loaded into the Black Maria and will be transported to jail. More arrests should follow. Mr. Morgan was the head of a robbery gang who hit railroad cars and stored the goods in the basement of the theater." He nodded toward Felix. "The Pinkertons have been assisting in surveillance."

Callum approached the sheriff. "Can you tell me for sure the lass is out of danger now?" He passed along the confiscated guns to the lawman.

"Yes, Mr. Morgan will be in jail a long time." He glanced around the room. "You can all stay here tonight, but tomorrow we're securing the dwelling until after his trial." He nodded toward Homer, Bessie, and Rose. "You folks will need to get your things out in the morning and find someplace else to stay."

He spoke to Rose. "Miss O'Brien, you have some admirers waiting for you on the front lawn."

Chapter Fifteen

Rose leaned against the Scotsman as he guided her down the stairs of the mansion she'd called home for the early part of her adult life. The man had rescued her twice, and by the hold around her waist, she'd have trouble escaping him again. They exited the house to the cheers, whoops, and hollers of the miners, railroad workers, and businessmen she'd entertained in the Five Star Saloon. She escaped his embrace, put her hand over her heart, and bowed to the men.

Mr. O'Donnell approached her, hat in hand. "Miss Rose." He dipped his head in respect. "I, as spokesmen for the group, am happy to see you are well and in good hands. If Callum, Doc, and Russ failed, we were ready to step up to the job. No one hurts our Songbird and gets away with it."

She gazed at the sincere faces of the men gathered around. The knowledge they would have given their lives caused a tear to slip down her face. She presented them with a sincere smile. "I've performed for heads of state and enjoyed standing ovations by audiences for my singing and acting, but I've never met such a fine group of gentlemen. You welcomed me to your town and now you cared enough to worry about my safety. God bless you all and know I love each and every one of you."

Rose shook hands with the men as they wandered

forward and told her how happy they were she was safe. She smiled and chatted with each one until they all mounted their rides and headed back to Wylder.

Rose and Callum watched the Wylder men ride into the night. "There must have been twenty people from the saloon." She held her hands over her heart and smiled.

"Twenty-five if you count Sonny and Boone. Counted them all." He stepped aside and let her walk ahead of him. "They care about you very much."

They entered the front room with the others. Rose sat on the settee and noticed the liquor stain on the rug. Thank God Mrs. Adams had the gumption to drug Walker. The older lady was full of vim and vigor. Her husband, Homer, was strong from all the hard work he'd done but they both faced an uncertain future. What would happen to them now?

Bessie poured a spot of tea into a cup and passed it to Rose. "How are you feeling? Your complexion is a little pale."

Doc Sullivan sat on the settee and studied her. "After your tea, I want to examine you and clean the cut on your face. Are you in any pain?"

"No." The symptoms of her stomach ailment were on the tip of her tongue, but she chose to not mention it. "I got knocked around a bit, but I don't think I have any more injuries."

Callum crossed his hands over his chest. "I want the lass to have a full examination. Had I known the way Willard Clayton treated her, I would have beat him instead of just knocking him out."

Rose stared up at the giant of a man and recognized the truth in his eyes. He'd fight to the death to protect her, and it made her heart expand in her chest. "Thank you, Callum, but it wasn't as bad as you men are making it out. I'm fine, or I will be after a good night's sleep."

Bessie collected cups and placed them on the tray. "I have rooms ready for you all upstairs. Make yourselves at home, and I'll have a good breakfast for everyone before you leave for Wylder."

Coyote helped Rose stand. "Miss Bessie, would you get some fresh water and clean cloths so I can tend the Songbird's wound? And please assist, if you don't mind."

"I don't mind at all." Bessie lifted the tray and made her way to the kitchen.

Callum guided Rose upstairs. "I know you're worried about Homer and Bessie. I'll talk to Daniel about them living at the ranch. Sarah will need some help with the little one, and we could use an extra hand taking care of the farm animals."

"Where will they live?" She never dreamed the Scotsman would be so generous.

"Right now, they'll stay at Culpepper's if she has a room. I'll go to the ranch and get the wagon and buggy. Russ already volunteered to help, and we'll take your belongings to Wylder tomorrow. You won't ever have to come back to this house again." They stopped at the entrance to her bedroom.

She examined his face and gazed into his blue eyes. His thick reddish-brown hair needed combing and his shirt had a tear on the sleeve. "Callum MacPhilip, you are the kindest man I've ever known."

He kissed her on the forehead and placed his hands on her shoulders. "Go on, lass. Let Doc Sullivan check you out."

Bessie hurried into the room with supplies, and Coyote closed the door. "Now, Miss O'Brien. Let's see to the cut on your face first." He cleaned the wound and applied ointment to the cut. "You won't need stitches. Take off your dress and let's check for any bruises or cuts on your body." Coyote turned his back and placed the soiled rags on a tray.

Rose allowed Bessie to undress her. "I've had a stomachache and nausea for the last few days, but only in the mornings and then I'm fine. I have been a little more tired and I think I've lost some weight, but I reckon that's from throwing up. I think I ate something bad." She lay on the bed, and Bessie placed a sheet over her.

Coyote and Bessie exchanged a glance. Doc crossed his arms over his chest and gazed down. "When was your last monthly?"

Rose pondered on the question. "The courses came this month when due, but it was strange. I spotted a little, unlike my usual. What's wrong? Do you think I'm gravely ill?"

Doc Sullivan sat in the chair beside the bed and Bessie busied herself with the cloth and bandages. "I need to examine you further, but I think you may be with child."

She swung her legs to the side of the bed and sat straight, holding the sheet around her body. "I can't. I'm thirty years old and have been unable to conceive in the past. It's impossible."

Doc rested his chin on his hand. "Sometimes it's not the woman's fault. I don't mean to be disconcerting toward your reputation, but it could have been caused by the man's infertility."

She stood beside the bed, her arms crossed along her chest to keep the covering from falling to the floor. "I give you permission to examine me."

He nodded to Bessie, who assisted Rose to the bed. After a thorough examination, Coyote covered her with a quilt and sat. "Miss O'Brien, you are with child."

The words the doc spoke bounced around the room for several seconds until they entered her ears and several more seconds before her brain connected with the utterance. "I'm going to have a baby?" The hoping, praying, promise to God, and then the disappointment each month pierced her heart and she cried, her body racked in sobs and her tears soaked the sheet.

"Rose, are you all right?" Coyote put his hands on her shoulders.

After thanking Saint Jude, the saint of desperate cases, she wiped the tears away with the towel Bessie passed her and smiled. "I've wanted a child for so many years, and I know now why God didn't answer my prayer." She wanted to tell Callum the news, he'd be happy and have her at the church tomorrow, but she didn't want their life together to start in that fashion. She wanted him to marry her because he loved her, not because he was obligated. "Please, don't tell Mr. MacPhilip. I'll tell him soon but not now, please both of you. Promise me."

Doc Sullivan walked toward the door. "You can count on my discretion."

Rose snuggled the cover under her chin. "Tell Callum I'm tired and ready for sleep. I'll see him in the morning."

"Sure thing, Miss O'Brien." Coyote exited her

room and eased the door shut.

Bessie sat on the bed and gathered Rose in an embrace. "My precious little woman. I am so happy for you and the Scotsman, but don't wait too long to tell him."

She rested her head on the lady's shoulder and breathed in the scent of lavender and sage. "I don't want to force any man to marry me. I can take care of myself and the child if need be."

Bessie tucked the covers around Rose. "Nonsense, I've never seen a man as smitten as your Callum is with you. You have a lot to digest, and it's been a very trying day. Everything will be better in the morning, dear." She removed a nightgown from the bureau. "Put this on and rest."

She stood beside the bed and allowed the lady to dress her. Her heart erupted with love for the child growing in her belly as her brain struggled to come to terms with the events of this day. She hugged her friend. "Thank you, Bessie. Good night."

The lady snuffed the candles and the kerosene lamp and tiptoed out of the room.

****

Sunshine streaked through the thin curtain, sending a glare into Rose's half-opened eyes. Remembrance of Doc Sullivan's diagnosis forced her awake, and she jumped out of bed and lurched toward the bowl and pitcher. Her body heaved and convulsed in an attempt to rid itself of everything she'd eaten in her thirty years of life. She reminded herself to ask the doctor how long the sickness would last. Would it be the entire time? The knowledge of her condition helped to ease the discomfort. She'd endure anything to deliver a healthy baby. She poured water on a rag and wiped her neck. Her reflection in the mirror showed a tired, pale, and ashen face staring back. Her hand fell to her still flat stomach, and she said good morning to the little life growing in her. She grabbed the rosary beads and held on to furniture to steady herself as she made her way to the rocking chair where she sat and thanked God, the Blessed Virgin Mary, and all the Saints for this miracle.

Bessie entered her room with a tray and placed it on the table. "Here's some ginger tea and toasted bread."

Rose set aside the beads and accepted the cup the woman passed her. "This is what I needed." Her hand shook as she held the cup and saucer, splashing some of the hot tea on her nightgown.

"Figured as much." Bessie sat on the edge of the bed and passed her a napkin. "The men left early this morning. Callum says he and Russ will come back soon to take us to Wylder. Homer and I are beside ourselves. We are thankful to be able to leave Cheyenne. So many bad memories for us."

Rose nibbled on a piece of bread. "This is a second chance for the two of you."

The old woman straightened the bedclothes. "And a new life for you and the little one." She placed clean clothes on the bed. "Your gentleman is very worried. He was hesitant to leave this morning, but I assured him you'd be safe with Homer and me until he returns."

Rose held her hair on the top of her head while Bessie fastened the buttons on the back of her dress. "He's worried over me since the day he found me in the snowstorm." Another cry swept through her throat but this one from happiness and the love for the kind man

139

and his seed growing inside her.

Chapter Sixteen

It was almost noon when Callum parked the large wagon outside the Cheyenne mansion. Russ parked beside him in Daniel's buggy. Doc Sullivan had returned to Wylder to see to any doctoring needed by the town folk. Callum thanked the man for his willingness to rescue Rose with a wife and wee *bairn* at home. The doc's experience in the war had given him the nickname Coyote, and he sure worked his magic last night by getting into the mansion unnoticed so they could take down the sentinels. It took all his reserve not to march in the house and tote his woman to the nearest church, marry her, and be done with it. *Shite*, she was a stubborn Irish lass. After a discussion with Russ, who knew a thing or two about stubborn women, specifically Miss Adelaide Willowby, he'd decided to step back and give the lass time to come to terms with the happenings of the last few days.

Homer Adams descended the porch steps. "Gentlemen." He carried a bag of clothes to the wagon. "We have several trunks. We're taking our clothes and personal belongings. The missus has been busy all morning."

"How is Rose?" The Scotsman hefted the bag to the buckboard.

"The wife said the girl was exhausted, so we let her sleep as long as we could. Bessie's upstairs with her

141

now getting her things together." He scooted a large box to the porch edge.

Callum and Russ made quick work putting the trunks in the wagon while Homer gave the horses fresh water.

The men climbed the stairs to the suite of rooms to get more baggage. Callum entered Rose's bedroom and stopped dead still. His lass appeared sick. She washed her face with a cloth and Bessie threw a towel over the basin bowl. He didn't hesitate or apologize, he gathered her in his arms. "*Mo ghràdh*, ye be sick this morning?"

She gazed into his eyes. "Must have been too much excitement."

"Of course, it has, lass." Walker Morgan was lucky to be in jail or he would be a dead man. "Will ye be able to make the trip in the buggy to Wylder?"

"Yes, one more cup of Bessie's tea, and I'll be fine." She sat in a chair.

The men loaded trunks and bags into the wagon and tied ropes around the belongings.

After a snack of bread, cheese, ham, and apples, the Scotsman placed the women in the buggy and drove the wagon to Wylder with Homer. He was thankful Morgan and his men were in jail but worried about Rose's health and safety. She deserved so much more than a little room at Culpepper's and singing at the saloon. When she recovered from this terror, he'd marry her and give her the love, home, and security she'd not known since her parents' death. And he would not take no for an answer.

The afternoon sun was falling toward the west by the time they arrived at the boarding house. He'd sent money with Doc for Homer and Bessie's room and wasn't surprised when Eulalie met them at the wagon.

The owner introduced herself to the Adamses. "Welcome to Wylder, I have your room ready." She spoke to Callum and Russ. "Follow me with their bags."

Homer dug in his vest pocket for money. "How much is our board for the week?"

"Mr. MacPhilip took care of it." She waved them off with her hand and entered her establishment.

"Thank you, Callum." Mr. Adams stepped toward him. "I'll repay you."

The Scotsman nodded and unloaded trunks and bags while Rose accompanied her friends to their new home.

Russ placed a box on the porch. "Going to say hello to Miss Addie and then I'll take the buggy back to Daniel."

"I'll not be far behind. Got work to do on the ranch before sundown. I've left too much for Daniel the last few weeks." Callum and Russ carried a heavy trunk to Rose's room.

The tasks done; Russ shook Homer's hand. "Best of luck to you and the missus. You'll like it in Wylder."

"The sheer stress of living in the home of a devil has done its toll on us both. Wylder is a small comfortable town and everyone we've met has been nice down-home folk." Homer pulled money from his pocket. "How much do I owe you, Callum?"

"Nothing. Call this a thank you for all you did for the lass through the years." He followed the man upstairs and bid him farewell in front of Rose's door. "Gonna say goodbye and get back to the ranch."

The man nodded. "We'll keep watch over your

girl."

"Thank you." He knocked and called out. "Bonnie lass, it's me."

She allowed his entry. "Did you get any sleep last night? You must be exhausted moving us and getting us to safety." She held his hands in hers and gazed into his eyes. "I owe you, Russ, and Coyote so much for risking your lives. Walker's men could have killed you." She rested her head on his chest.

He breathed in the smell of a rose garden lingering in her hair, dipped his head, and found her mouth brushing soft kisses on her full lips. Her whimper made him deepen the kiss and draw her so close their bodies melded together as one. How he wanted to make slow love from now until the morning. He reprimanded himself for not thinking of her first. She'd been sick and needed time to recover. He placed a chaste kiss on her cheek and cradled her in his arms. "Are ye working tonight?"

"No, I sent word to Boone I'll return tomorrow." She snuggled close.

"Good." He put his finger under her chin and lifted her face. "I love ye, Rose." She didn't respond but the smile on her face and the light in her eyes gave him hope.

Laughter bubbled from her throat. "You could open a business and call it 'The Scotsman, rescuing damsels in distress since 1879.' "

"Only you, my love." He entered the dark hall and trekked down the stairs to the waiting wagon.

Callum returned to the ranch, settled the team of horses in the barn and started mucking out the stables. He was behind on so many things, and he swore he'd make everything right. His life had been in upheaval since the day he found Songbird on the road to Wylder. When he was at the ranch, he fretted over her in town, and when he was in town he worried over his duties at the ranch. This was the worst time to be distracted. Daniel needed him more than ever, since Sarah's due date approached. He continued to work until the dinner bell rang. Sarah had made it a rule if she had enough food to share at supper, she'd ring the bell.

He brushed hay off his clothes and washed his hands in a bucket and headed to the big house.

Sarah opened the back door to let him enter and wobbled to the stove. "I made mutton stew for supper. How is Rose?"

Callum escorted her to a chair. "Sit, let me prepare the food." He assisted her and scooted her chair to the table. "She's tired and wasn't feeling well this morning, so I left her in town with Homer and Bessie Adams." He set the table with bowls, spoons, and a large pot of stew.

"Homer and Bessie Adams? Who are they?" Sarah closed her eyes and rubbed her belly, taking a deep breath and letting it out.

"They lived…"

Daniel entered the kitchen and kissed his wife on the cheek. "Smells good in here."

Everyone sat at the table and bowed their heads for Daniel to say the blessing over the food.

Callum spooned stew into Sarah's bowl and answered her question. "Homer and Bessie Adams lived in Walker Morgan's home. She was his housekeeper and cook and Homer, the butler, did odd jobs around the house. They're in their late fifties." He filled his bowl and continued. "I got them a room at Eulalie's, but they'll need work."

Daniel squeezed Sarah's hand. "We could use some help, with the baby coming. Sarah wants to continue to do her embroidery, so she'll need someone to help with the baby and house cleaning. You and I could use an extra person to take care of the farm animals and keep the grounds so we can concentrate on our growing horse population."

"I hoped you would consent to them living here and working for us." Callum tore off a piece of bread and dipped it in his stew.

Sarah wiped her face with her napkin. "That would be wonderful but…"

"But what?" Daniel spooned stew in his mouth.

"Where will they stay?" She drank a sip of milk. "I don't want to be rude. I grew up with a housekeeper living in our home, but I've grown accustomed to just being the two of us and now our child. I guess I'm jealous and don't want to share all my time with anyone but my family."

Callum said, "I understand, I feel the same." He addressed his friend. "If they'll take the position, we'll build them a house and they can work for both of us. We can split their salaries."

"Excellent idea." Daniel broke a biscuit in half. "Bessie may need some classes in how to cook biscuits, scones, and stew."

Callum winked at Sarah. "I taught Sarah; guess I can teach Mrs. Adams."

Sarah shook her head. "Jake gave me my first cooking classes, but I think your scone recipe is what made my husband marry me."

Daniel's chuckles filled the room. "Yes, dear, it was your delicious scones and not the fact I fell in love with you the first moment I laid eyes on you dressed in your fine clothes fighting off Silus and Jasper Nelson the day you arrived in Wylder."

The Scotsman's grin stretched across his face as he stared at the two lovebirds and remembered how Daniel had almost lost her twice, once to the kidnappers and her father when he rode the train to Wylder to take her home. "It's settled then. I'll talk to them tomorrow and offer the position."

Chapter Seventeen

Rose drifted to sleep as soon as her head hit the pillow and slept until the sun beamed in her window. As soon as her eyes opened, she ran to the bowl and the now-familiar morning sickness. She poured water on a towel and wet her face. A light knock and Bessie's voice was a welcoming sound. She opened the door, her stomach still roiling with nausea. "Come in." She stepped aside, rubbing her neck with the wet cloth.

Mrs. Adams entered with a tray of ginger tea and hard bread. "This will make you better."

Rose cleared a spot on the table for the food. "Thank you so much, Miss Bessie."

The older lady poured tea into the cup and passed it. "You didn't make it down for breakfast so I asked Eulalie if I could deliver it to you."

"Is that so?" Her voice lilted in disbelief. "Eulalie Culpepper allowed you to bring my breakfast to me on a tray?"

"Um, yes. We had a delightful breakfast which I'm sure you don't want to hear about and an interesting conversation." She gave Rose the small plate with bread. "Miss Culpepper and the entire town of Wylder have welcomed us, and we could not be happier. And Callum, paying our first week's board, and all he's done for us—you have a jewel of a man."

"Yes, he is one of a kind." She nibbled on the

bread and drank all the tea.

Bessie gathered the dishes. "I need to get these back to Eulalie, and Homer wants me to stroll with him around town. He's going to see what kind of job he can find."

Rose almost mentioned Callum's offer but wasn't sure Daniel and Sarah would be interested. "I'll get dressed and find you." Her small room was filled with her extra trunk and satchels full of clothes. She'd not taken any of the expensive jewelry Walker had given her and wanted nothing to remind her of their time together. She longed to luxuriate in a warm bath but had to settle on a quick toilette and a comfortable cotton dress.

She stared in her mirror, adjusting her straw hat, when a knock rang out. Rose opened the door expecting Bessie had forgotten something. A beautiful young woman with a baby stood before her. "You must have the wrong room." She started to close the door, but the lady's words halted her action.

"Miss Rose O'Brien?" The girl said as she bounced the bundle in her arms.

"Yes, I'm Rose O'Brien."

"I'm Eliza Jane Sullivan, Samuel's wife." She gave a proud smile. "May I come in?"

"Samuel?" Rose stuttered.

"Doctor Samuel Coyote Sullivan." She entered the room.

Rose tossed clothes from the chair. "I'm so sorry about this room. These are my belongings from Cheyenne, and I have no place to put them."

"I understand." Eliza removed the blanket to show her baby's face. "This is Little Sam." She held the boy so Rose could see his face. "He is the spitting image of my Coyote."

She stared at the precious child. He was beautiful and perfect. A tear slid from her eye, and she wiped it away. "Please sit."

Her new friend sat in the chair and cradled the baby on her arm. "Coyote told me about your condition. I know you want to keep it a secret for now. I can keep a confidence; it comes with being a doctor's wife. He wanted me to visit with you and see if you have any questions."

Questions? If she asked all she wanted to know, Eliza wouldn't be home for supper. "Were you sick in the mornings?" She sat on the bed.

"I had morning sickness into my twelfth week. Are you drinking ginger tea?" She smiled down at her sleeping baby.

"Yes, seems to help the most." Rose wrung her hands. "I feel better later in the day, and then I'm so hungry."

"I was the same. When your precious bundle comes, you won't remember the nausea or the pain of the delivery, trust me." She handed the baby to Rose.

"This is the second time I've held a baby." The infant didn't wake, he snuggled against her body. For the first time since Doc told her she was with child, she accepted the truth, and joy overflowed, replacing the blood in her veins with hope. She smiled at the infant, but her chin quivered, and tears escaped her eyes. "I thought I was barren." A jagged breath filled her lungs. "I've prayed and prayed and even begged God for a baby."

Eliza touched her shoulder. "You have a strong

womb, but the gentleman's seed wasn't. God answered your prayer and sent the man he wanted you to have."

Rose closed her eyes and thanked St. Jude for interceding and giving her the desire of her heart. She passed the baby back to his mother. "Any advice you want to share?"

The mother stood and cradled the child over her shoulder. "Yes." She raised her head and gave a very serious reply. "Don't let everyone treat you like a porcelain doll because you're expecting. We're stronger than men think we are. If we weren't, God would have chosen the men to give birth."

Rose gave the young woman a huge smile. "I like you, Eliza Jane. I think we are going to be great friends."

"You are just as gracious and nice as Samuel said you were. I'm on my way to see my mother at the Social Club if you want to accompany me." Eliza sauntered toward the door.

Rose never expected to hear the word mother and Social Club used in a sentence. "Who is your mother?"

"Miss Adelaide Willowby. She loves her grandbaby." She swaddled the baby boy on her shoulder.

"No, I don't want to run into Amethyst." Rose opened the door.

"I understand. We've got lots to discuss, so I'll see you soon." Eliza hesitated. "This isn't advice, it's a fact. That Scotsman loves you."

"Yes, he does, and I love him." She touched the baby's back. The smallness of his body combined with the softness made her ache to feel the touch of her child. "I'll do right by him."

"I'm glad." She walked into the hall. "And Rose…"

"Yes?"

"Welcome to Wylder."

Rose donned her riding clothes and hurried to the livery. She wouldn't let another day go by before she told Callum her news.

Chet pounded horseshoes on his anvil and stopped at her approach. "Good morning, Miss O'Brien."

"Morning, Mr. Daniels. Will you assist me with my saddle? I want to ride a bit." She waited for him to set aside his hammer and tongs.

"Of course." Chet wiped his hands on his apron and followed her to Daisy's stall. "If you don't mind me asking, where do you plan to ride?"

Her eyes narrowed and her first response was *None of your business*, but she gave him a slight smile.

He grabbed her saddle and added, "Mr. MacPhilip understands you enjoy riding, but he wanted me to keep an eye on you." He hurried with his explanation. "Well, after all that's happened to you." He let out a breath. "I'm sorry, miss, but the entire town wants to keep you safe."

The entire town, her little town, Wylder, Wyoming. Not since her parents died had she belonged anywhere. "I'm going to ride out to the Lex Taylor. I need to see Mr. MacPhilip."

He entered Daisy's stall. "I can accompany you."

"No, I'll be fine." She patted her horse as the blacksmith readied her pet.

Rose talked to Daisy as they rode to the ranch, telling her about her condition and how they would stay in Wylder and maybe even have a home with Callum.

He'd asked her to marry him, but she'd refused and worried he'd changed his mind.

She pulled back the reins and guided Daisy into the lane headed to the ranch. She paused before the arch and reflected on the time she'd spent here, safe, loved, and taken care of. Callum had seen to that from the moment he rescued her and Daisy. She gazed at the mountains in the distance and prayed he still wanted her. This land was the home of her valiant man, her rescuer, her equal. She dug her heels into Daisy's side and hurried to the barn. She dismounted and tied the horse's reins to a hitching post near the water trough.

Yellow wildflowers swayed in the breeze. She picked one and rounded the corner of the barn toward the arena. Callum worked a horse with intense concentration. He'd not seen her approach, and she marveled at his patience with the animal. His fluid movements reminded her of a dance as he waltzed with the stallion backward and forward until the horse's legs waltzed in time with his. He spoke to the animal and removed the bridle.

He saw Rose approach and hurried toward her. "Is everything all right? Did you come out here by yourself?"

She prodded toward him, and they leaned against the wooden fence. "Yes, Daisy's at the barn." She leaned toward him and rested her head on his chest to gather strength from him before she spoke.

"I've missed you, lass." He kissed her lips and smoothed her hair falling from underneath her straw hat. "Are you going to tell me you've got your train ticket to California?"

"California?" Her well-made plans now seemed so

foreign. "How did you know?"

"Boone." Callum inhaled a deep breath. "I don't want you to go."

She closed her eyes and put her arms around his neck. "I don't want to go. I could never live anywhere and not see your face every day." She tiptoed and kissed him. He deepened the kiss and groaned. His secure arms lifted her, and her feet dangled in the air as they kissed as if nothing would ever come between them again.

He released her and positioned her so her back was to the fence. He got down on one knee and took her hand in his. "Rose O'Brien. Will you please marry me?"

Her chin quivered as it always did when she was about to cry. Her hands fisted, and she smiled to keep the sobs away. "Yes, Callum MacPhilip. I will marry you and the three of us will be a family."

"Three of us?" He used the fence post for leverage and stood. "You, me, and…"

"A baby." Rose laughed as tears ran down her face. "I'm with child, Callum. Your child."

"A *bairn*." He gathered her in his arms and swung her around.

"Stop." She wiggled free. "Put me down, you're going to make me dizzy."

He released her to the ground. "I'm sorry, lass." He put his hands on each side of her face. "Are ye well?"

She raised the flower and sniffed the sweet scent while watching the horses graze in the pasture. "I'm ill every morning when I wake, but Doc says it's normal."

"Coyote didn't tell me." The Scotsman put his hands on his hips. "I'll have his hide."

Rose crossed her hands over her chest. "Now, Callum MacPhilip, we need to get some things straight. I made Doc promise not to tell you. It was between me and you, and I wanted to tell you myself. And another thing, you are a pig-headed man, and we are not going to start our marriage with you telling me what to do and getting mad if I don't do it."

He picked her up and started toward the house. "I should have known better than to fall in love with a stubborn Irish lass. If you think we're going to start our marriage by you telling me what to do and keeping things from me, well, you've got another thing coming."

She struggled to free herself. "Put me down.".

"No." He continued toward his cabin. "I'm going to spank you like I will our *bairns* when they need it."

"Children? You seem to think there will be more?" She kicked her legs to no avail. "And you are not going to spank me like a bad child." She relaxed and gazed into the Scotsman's face. A twinkle from his blue eyes and the grin on his face told her he would never hurt her. She'd learned his temper flamed quick but never lasted, unlike hers which could last for days. There was so much to learn about this man, and she couldn't wait to start.

He opened the door with her still in his arms and carried her to his bedroom. "You are more than a wife, you are *mo chridhe*. As soon as we arrange it with Father Brandon, it will be official, but for now, I'm going to love you as a husband loves a wife."

Rose tiptoed, removed his hat, and ran her fingers through his wild hair. "Callum, you have always loved me that way."

"Aye, lass. And I always will."

His lips found hers and he let out a sigh. He put his hands on each side of her face and stared into her eyes. "I've loved ye since the first day I laid my eyes on you in Cheyenne near a year ago."

"I remember." A smile bloomed on her face.

"I *didnae ken* ye noticed me." He scooped her in his arms and placed her on the bed. "My bonnie lass, had I known of your troubles, I'd have stolen you away the moment my eyes beheld you in Cheyenne." He sat in the chair and removed his boots and pants. "Ye be mine, Rose, and I'll not let another come between us."

She removed the pin from her hair and let the tresses fall around her shoulders. "Am I correct in the assumption you will never go to the Social Club?" She removed her dress and draped it on a chair.

"Aye, I'll never need to go to the Social Club." Callum threw his shirt on the floor. "And will ye not sing at the saloon?"

She placed her hands on his bare chest. "You would be correct." She led him to their bed.

"Ye have on too many clothes." He tugged her chemise over her head and drew her close, their bare skin touching. "*Mo chridhe*." He kissed her mouth and whispered. "You will always be my heart."

Chapter Eighteen

Rose opened her bedroom window and stared at the clear blue sky. Her gaze drifted down as the chickens cackled and scratched the ground for food. Eulalie's cook stepped around them as she gathered eggs from their roosts and placed them in her basket. This was the last morning she would spend in the boarding house.

She'd risen at dawn to pack and organize her things. The sickness had arrived as it did each morning, but she refused to let it interfere with her wedding day. Her white dress lay on the bed along with the plaid fabric of gray, blue, red, and black Callum requested she tie around her waist. He told her it was the color of his Highland clan's tartan.

She'd never seen him in fancy clothes and couldn't imagine her Scotsman in anything but his denim pants and brown shirt.

A loud knock sounded, and Bessie's voice sang out in a lilting tone, "Rose, my love. I've come to get you ready for your day."

She welcomed her friend inside. The groom had taken care of the specifics of their special day and offered Homer and Bessie work on the ranch which they accepted. "Thank you for helping me. Seems all I've done is pace around this room, a nervous bundle of energy, not knowing what to do."

"Of course, you'd be anxious on your wedding day." The lady helped her dress, then combed and arranged her hair, securing the front of Rose's long red tresses on top of her head with a silver comb, and brushed the back of her hair allowing it to curl along her back. "Hair is done, stand up for me." Bessie tied the plaid fabric around her waist. "Homer and I love you like you were ours."

Rose dabbed her eye with her lace handkerchief. "And I love you both. I'm grateful you chose to live on the ranch with us. We can be a family and my little ones will have grandparents."

"They will." Bessie gave the bride her parasol and reticule. "Now on to the church. Chet Daniels should be here with his buggy about now."

The women waited outside the church. The old lady smoothed Rose's hair and adjusted the plaid tartan. "I've never seen such a beautiful bride."

Rose hugged her friend and they walked inside. Her Scotsman stood at the altar with Father Brandon. He wore a kilt made from the same cloth as the one around her waist, black socks to his knee, and a black and silver sporran around his waist. His short coat was buttoned, and he sported a light blue shirt underneath. My, he was a handsome Scotsman dressed in the uniform of his clan. She put her hand over her heart and caught her breath. She never dreamed he'd be dressed in a kilt.

A smile overtook her entire face as she realized she, Rose O'Brien, was marrying a Scottish Highlander. They may have traveled an ocean to find each other in Wyoming but she was still an Irish lass and he the burly Scotsman who'd stolen her heart with a glance.

Together they would raise a family and make a home in Wylder, Wyoming.

A word about the author…

Jane Lewis dreamed of being a romance writer since she read her first romance novel. She wrote articles for her school newspaper, articles for a music magazine, and composed and arranged music. When she isn't writing, re-writing, or editing her next romance novel, she enjoys cooking, playing music, yoga, weight training, and hanging out with her real-life hero, her husband.

She is a member of Romance Writers of America and Georgia Romance Writers. She was a 2016 finalist in the Hearts Through History, Post-Victorian/World War II category for her first romance novel, *Love At Five Thousand Feet*. *The Lady Flyer* was awarded second place in the North Texas Romance Writers of America Carolyn Reader's Choice Awards in 2021.